Vengeful CONspiracies

A Sadie Sabatini Mystery
Book 2

Nicole Leiren

ISBN: 978-1-963705-12-6

Published in the United States of America by Harbor Lane Books, LLC.

www.harborlanebooks.com

This book is dedicated to my beautiful daughter. Her fierce protection of those around her has helped inspire the character of Sadie. Her love of reading and the excitement she has when sharing the plot of whatever story she's immersed in helps me remember why I spend time in a writing cave. Thank you, Babygirl, for being the amazing person you are!

Chapter One

Today was going to be a great day. How could it not be when it started with kayaking on beautiful Lake Amore as the sun rose in the east. Peace filled my soul with each stroke. Lake Amore was one of the largest manmade lakes in Texas. Starting my new life here on this little peninsula was the right decision. Since moving here, I'd been graced with a lakefront home, a business that honored the heritage of my father, new friends, and a handsome man. All right, I could probably ask for more when it came to the handsome man, as he remained solidly in the friend zone. I'm a patient woman, though, and I held out hope there might be more in the future.

Six months ago, I'd hit the reset button and closed the door on a past filled with righting as many wrongs as my team and I could manage in the decade or so we'd been running cons for the greater good rather than our own personal gain.

As I maneuvered the kayak into the dock attached to the back of my property, I admitted to myself there had been some material rewards for our efforts as well. It hadn't been our main goal, but it had been a karma-inspired result for taking on the cases Lady Justice had not only been blind to but had turned her back on completely. Of course, sometimes karma returned to exact justice of its own kind. I'd already experienced that once and prayed my penance was now complete.

I made myself a cappuccino and enjoyed every sip before heading into the storefront I owned. Tesoro, Italian for treasure, was the venture I'd undertaken to start my new life. Venetian blown glass transformed into jewelry, glassware, and pieces of art designed to capture everyone's attention was my passion now. I loved being surrounded by such beauty every day and, after a rocky start, others in the town were starting to appreciate it, too. I wasn't making a profit yet, but it was okay. Money wouldn't be an issue for quite some time to come.

Tesoro opened promptly at ten in the morning, and my first visitor arrived around noon. "Hi, Kelsey," I greeted my nearest and dearest friend here in Wilson. She'd stood by me from the beginning. She hadn't bailed when things got dicey right after I moved in, so she'd earned my friendship and, most importantly, my trust.

"Hi, Sadie. Have you been busy this morning?" She moved around the shop, admiring the newest items on display.

"No, but on a Friday, things don't typically pick up until the afternoon."

She turned to me with a twinkle in her emerald eyes. "Excited about your date tonight with Jeremy?"

"It's not a date," I corrected her. "We're just friends having dinner together."

"Mmm hmm." She emphasized her response with a waggling of her auburn eyebrows. "The two of you have had dinners on and off for the last couple of months. How is it not a date?"

The sigh wanting to escape my heart stopped somewhere in my throat. This was the part of our relationship that saddened me the most. Because of my past and the danger it could pose, I couldn't tell her the truth, the whole truth, and nothing but the truth. I feared if she knew about it, her potential disappointment could end what had blossomed into a beautiful friendship. Her dismay wouldn't come from what I'd tried to do, but the way I'd chosen to do it. I had no regrets. I'd always been a means-justifies-the-end kind of gal. Understandably, not everyone saw life like that. As a result, it was a dilemma I'd encountered multiple times already. I smiled obligingly in her direction. "We've agreed we enjoy each other's company, but neither is ready for anything beyond that. As my friend, can you understand and respect that?"

My words had their desired effect. She moved over and pulled me into a hug. "Of course. You just seem so happy when you're with him. It seemed natural to me that you two might want to be together. I'm sorry."

"No apology necessary. Now, enough of that talk. Let's change the subject."

"Okay. So, you're coming with me to the Meet The Candidate event on Sunday night, right?"

"You've not given me much choice," I teased. "Why is this such a big deal?"

The eye roll and dramatic sigh she leveled in my direction made me smile. "Because..." She drew out the word. "This is an unprecedented election with three of the five seats up for re-election."

It did sound significant. I'd never taken part much in local politics unless it was necessary to take down a dirty politician. But I'd promised myself to try new things and could think of no valid reason—well, none that Kelsey would let me get away with—to not go. "Of course, I'll be there."

She offered me a quick embrace. "Okay, gotta run. Pete and I have dinner plans tonight as well. We're celebrating the referral fee he's going to get from bringing in a big business deal. You have to love luck that puts you at the right place and right time. Pete ran into this man at the club, they shared some nice tequila, and he got him to agree to select his firm to broker the deal."

It made me wonder if it was luck or if Pete had heard through the grapevine where the guy was going to be and planned a way to nab this big fish. Either way, props to him for taking the initiative. "Was it someone from Wilson, since they met at The Club?"

Kelsey nodded. "Yes, he's new in town, moved in

less than a month ago, and he's running for one of the spots on the board."

"Really? What are his chances, being the new kid in town?" I'd been the new kid in this small town a short time ago and experienced firsthand how hard it was to get people to trust, much less elect you to represent them.

"No idea, but that's what will make it even more interesting."

"What's his name?"

"Miles Gentry. Now, enough politics talk. I want to look closer at some of the new jewelry items."

"I can't argue with that. Let me know if you need any help."

While she browsed, I pulled a vanilla Greek yogurt from the mini fridge and stirred in some granola. Normally, I'd have something a little more substantial, but pasta was on my brain for tonight's dinner with Jeremy. This translated to yogurt for lunch, a sacrifice I willingly made.

I grabbed my laptop and returned to the counter. Since Kelsey didn't want to talk about the election now, I wouldn't bother her. I was curious, though, about the candidates. The seats being voted on were currently occupied by Jim Bob (JB) Nester, Alan Knightly, and Ted Birmingham. Ted was the only one not running for re-election. I was a little surprised by this. When it came to the Birminghams and their legacy, both influence and power were important. Since Ted typically did what his father wanted, I had no doubt it was Robert's idea.

Next, I wanted to take a look at the candidates running to occupy those seats. "Hey, Tessa is running."

Kelsey looked my way and grinned. "I knew you'd do some research before Sunday."

I shrugged. "The Boy Scouts and I have that in common—always be prepared. I've visited her shop, Tessa's Treats, many times."

"She will be a great asset to the board, for sure. One vote down, two to go." She winked.

Next up was Karen Bizzy, the "Karen" to beat out all other "Karens." She had definitive plans for the town of Wilson, very few of which I supported. Denise McDowell and Jackie Price were also vying for a seat. I wasn't sure either was truly qualified, but out of the two, I knew Denise better. Her motivations, at least, were easier to understand. Jackie, on the other hand, was still a mystery.

Since I was familiar with them, I hadn't selected the hyperlink under their name to see the bio and picture. The new guy, Miles Gentry, needed additional research. I hovered over the blue letters that contained his name and hit enter.

As his picture appeared on a new page, my heart stopped beating for a moment. His hair might no longer be black, and contacts had replaced his glasses, but the face struck a familiar chord from my past. This man was not Miles Gentry. No, I'd recognize the smug look on his narrow face anywhere. This was none other than Miles Grant, a former pharmaceutical executive my team brought down about a year ago due to his use of experimental pesticides which poisoned the workers in the field. He had also skimmed money from the company to fund other experimental programs. In sum, he was a bad actor who had either learned his lesson and was starting a new life, or he had moved from California to Texas to start a new venture where no one knew him or his reputation. At least, he would think no one knew him.

Either way, I didn't trust him. My gut was rarely, if ever, wrong. Right now, it was screaming at me that his presence in Wilson spelled bad news for the unsuspecting people of this town. Deep down, I also knew it wouldn't be long before our paths crossed, which undoubtedly would mean nothing but trouble for me.

Chapter Two

I closed the shop a little early. A few weekenders were in town and had stopped in to make some purchases. Wilson was made up of mostly retired and semi-retired couples. While there were a few children in the area, most of the younger people only showed up on the weekends when they came to visit grandparents. The rest of the population was made up of oil and gas executives or other wealthy individuals who commuted from Houston and the surrounding area for a change of pace. From the concrete jungle to the wooded lake, it wasn't hard to see the appeal.

Thankfully, business had been a little slow today. Normally, that might have bothered me and set my thoughts on my next advertising campaign or efforts to bring awareness to the beautiful items in my shop. But today, my thoughts were centered on Miles. I didn't want to wait until Sunday night to confront him at the candidate forum. My discussion with him needed to be private. If I'd learned anything since becoming a resident here, it was that the rumor mill operated pretty much twenty-four, seven. I'd provided enough fodder to feed that beast for a lifetime already, so there was no sense in renewing negative interest in myself again.

I surveyed my wardrobe choices for my 'non-date' and finally settled on a pair of gray slacks and a turquoise blouse. Nice, but not over the top. Jeremy and I were having dinner at The Club. Located in the heart of Wilson, right on the lake, it served as the epicenter for the town. Besides a wonderful bar and food selection, most of the community events from games to dances to hosting candidate forums occurred in this building. Along with a beautiful view, the mahogany furniture, linen tablecloths, stone walls, and high-beamed ceiling provided both a sense of comfort and affluence. You could dress up or down for happy hour or dinner. They'd somehow struck just the right balance to make everyone feel at home here.

Once ready, I reached for my phone to text Emerson. At fourteen years old, he was one of the few exceptions to children living in Wilson. Though, if he heard me refer to him as a child, he would be upset. His aunt, Isabella, who ran Wilson's Floral, had assumed guardianship of him when both of his parents were killed in a terrible boating accident. Emerson maintained it wasn't an accident, though. Jeremy, my non-date for the evening, served his community as a game warden for Crockett County, of which Wilson was a part. He sided with Emerson that something seemed off about the whole thing, but without any evidence, everyone had to accept that sometimes terrible things happened to good people.

Because of his status as one of the few young people in the area, everyone in town had adopted him and helped Isabella with his care. This meant he knew everyone and, if he didn't know something, he had a way of finding out. Pulling up his contact, I texted, *Hi, Emerson. You know about the new guy in town? Miles Gentry?*

In typical teenage fashion, his phone was never far from him, so his response came quickly. *A little, not here long enough to learn much. Why?*

His face looks familiar. I want to learn more before the forum.

Emerson knew more about local politics than eighty percent of the residents. His aspirations for the future included becoming chief of police. I was certain he'd already been doing his research ahead of Monday night's meeting. *What do you want to know?*

Where he lives in Wilson.

Let me check. I'll text you.

Thanks. Now, go have some teenage fun! I worried he'd grown up entirely too fast after the death of his parents, so I always encouraged him to enjoy his youth.

LOL I'll try. Enjoy your date with the game warden.

It was not a date, I sighed, but I refrained from sharing with Emerson. No need to explain my motives to a teenager, no matter how mature he might be.

Thirty minutes later, Jeremy looked as handsome as ever as he opened the door for me at The Club. His beautiful smile lit up those mesmerizing hazel eyes with golden flecks. I was certain one could get lost in that gorgeous gaze for a lifetime. I took a deep breath and exhaled slowly, reminding myself, *Just friends.*

The piano player provided the perfect background music for a relaxing evening. We'd just been seated and ordered our drinks–wine for me and sparkling water for him–when I noticed, out of the corner of my eye, two men being seated a few tables away. My fist clenched in my lap when recognizing one of the men as none other than Miles Gentry. Now, not only did this man hold the potential to ruin my new life, but my dinner as well.

"How was your day?" Jeremy asked with that smile of his that could melt butter with its warmth.

I refocused on him and returned the smile. "Another day, another dollar. How about yours?"

"You know, same ol' same ol'."

"Yes, it must be terrible riding around in your boat all day on a beautiful lake."

"Looking for violations and bad guys. You always forget that part."

I shrugged and took a sip of my wine. "I don't forget. I choose to ignore. There's a difference."

He laughed. "Noted. I'm glad we can enjoy this evening out. Starting Wednesday of next week, I'm covering the night shift for a buddy in the department. Last minute wedding, I guess."

The way he said it made me smile. "He has to make an honest woman out of her or something?"

The blush that crept over his sun-kissed cheeks broadened my smile. "Nothing like that. She's getting deployed and he wanted them to be official before she left."

My heart might have melted a little. "That's sweet and very romantic." Laughter from the table Miles was seated at drew my attention. The desire to confront him grew with each passing minute.

Jeremy laughed. "Or it could be that he wanted them to be able to have base housing when she returned."

That sounded more reasonable, even if not romance-book worthy. "All right, we'll opt for practical with a hint of sweetness."

"That works."

He sipped on his water for a moment before his smile faded. Since, with Jeremy, often I had no idea where his thought processes were headed other than in the opposite direction of mine, it was better to ask then speculate. "What's wrong?"

After a small sigh, he met my gaze. "I've noticed you keep looking at the men a couple tables over. Want to tell me what about them keeps your attention from our stimulating conversation?"

Apparently, I wasn't as good at multitasking as I thought. "I'm pretty sure I know one of them." I gestured with a nod of my head in his direction. It helped that there was no one seated at the tables between us.

"Who is he?"

"Depends on who you ask." It was an honest answer, but not one he would appreciate.

He leaned back. "Why is everything with you always so complicated?"

I took another sip of wine. "I know it is, and as much as I'd like to change that aspect about myself, I don't see my life becoming uncomplicated anytime soon."

"Well, at least you're honest." The server arrived in time to save me from responding. Honesty about my true self would be the one thing that ensured he and I never went on a non-date again.

We ordered, but despite trying to keep up with our conversation, whatever Miles and his companion were in deep discussion about kept drawing my attention. The other man looked to be in his late twenties or early thirtics. Jeremy's voice broke into my concentration. "Why don't you go say hello or whatever it is you need to do or say?"

"I'm sorry. This isn't how I wanted the evening to start out."

"Go, before our dinner arrives."

I knew if I didn't, I'd be sidetracked all evening and Jeremy would simply pay the check and go home. He liked me, but he didn't put up with any of my shenanigans, as he called them. He was a what-you-see-is-what-you-get kind of guy. I, on the other hand, was full of mystery and gray areas from his perspective. "Okay, thank you."

Once at their table, Miles looked up from his companion and our gazes locked. He knew. I knew. He stood and smiled. It looked like we were going to play nice–I could do that. "Good evening, gentlemen. My apologies for interrupting, but Miles, is that you?"

Miles extended his hand. "That's me, Miles Gentry, and this is my business partner, James Cutter."

I did not take the olive branch Miles shared. One could only pretend so much. Instead, I turned to James to shake his hand. He rose from his chair and clasped his hand in mine with a firm grip. "Nice to meet you, ma'am. How do you know Mr. Gentry?"

"Oh, we go back quite a way, wouldn't you say, Miles?"

"Yes, I suppose we do. Maybe we should catch up soon? James and I need to continue our discussion. I'm sure you want to get back to your date."

Again, there was no point in correcting him. I could sense the heat from my non-date's gaze as he watched our exchange. I should have agreed to talk with Miles later, in private. But it was usually a fifty-fifty chance I did what I should versus what my final choice reflected. And right now, my choice was to provide a warning to Mr. Cutter. "You should be very careful who you get into business with, sir. Rarely are people who they seem, especially when they're looking for sizable amounts of cash from you."

Miles laughed loudly, drawing more attention our way than I wanted. "You should know a lot about that."

"My intentions have always been and will continue to be honorable, Mr. Grant."

His tanned face turned a crimson red at my use of his former last name. He took a step toward me, but I was ready to defend myself. Before I had a chance to respond, Jeremy's body had moved between the two of us. Mr. Gentry/Grant got lucky my knee hadn't connected with his groin, which no doubt would have sent him to the floor until dessert arrived. "I think it's time to end this little reunion, don't you?" His steely gaze bore into Miles and, I admit, made me a little weak in the knees. My reaction, however, had little to do with fear.

We'd now garnered the attention of everyone dining that evening. Even the piano player had stopped to see what was going on. After a few moments, Miles exhaled slowly. "My apologies, Miss whatever your name is now."

Jeremy cut me a look but said nothing. Instead, he took my elbow and led me back to our table. "Care to explain?"

I really didn't. "It's a long story."

"Another person you pretended to be a journalist for? Did you want information from him, too, or something else?" Guess he hadn't completely forgiven my ruse the first time we met. I might have pretended to be someone else. Not my finest hour, for sure. To Jeremy's credit, it took him less than a day to figure it out. I was either losing my touch, or I really had it bad for him. Maybe both.

"Can we please not talk about this right now?"

He raised his hand and got the attention of our server. "We'll take our food to go, and I'll take the check."

"Yes, sir."

I crossed my arms. "Is that really necessary?"

"Yes."

And people wondered why I said we weren't dating. If we had been, the best case scenario was that this would've been a couple's fight. The worst case scenario was that we'd be breaking up. Either way, I was no happier than he was about this development.

With our to-go bags in hand, he walked me to my truck. I attempted to repair the damage. "Look, I know you tolerate my reticence about sharing details of my past. I wish it didn't have to be that way. I also know I've done nothing to truly earn your trust, but I'm asking you to believe me when I say that, for now, it's for the best. Until I can be sure nothing from my past can hurt anyone in my present, it's how I protect the people I care most about."

He sighed and leaned in to kiss me on the cheek. This was shaping up to be the worst non-date yet. "I promise to think about it, but that's it. I hope you understand."

Sadly, I did. "Of course. Can I call you sometime?"

He flashed me a quick smile. "I always take your calls, don't I?"

I nodded and leaned up to return his kiss on the cheek. "Thanks, Jeremy. Enjoy the rest of your night. And again, I'm sorry."

Once back at home, I put dinner in the fridge. After a hot bath and glass (or two) of wine, I turned in for the night. I couldn't have been asleep for more than a few hours when my phone rang. Shaking my head to clear the cobwebs clouding my brain, I answered, "Hello?"

"I'm gonna need you to come down to the station," a voice which sounded vaguely familiar directed.

"Who is this?"

There was a chuckle. "Deputy Matthews."

Ah, that explained why the annoying voice sounded so familiar. Deputy Jake Matthews had served as the bane of my existence when I arrived in town, and not much had occurred to change that. "What do you want?"

He laughed. "Well, truthfully, I'd like you to leave town as you've been nothing but trouble since you arrived."

My eyes rolled, even though they were still closed. "You've tried to run me out of town before and failed. Why don't you move on with your life?" I know, I know. I was baiting him, but it *was* the middle of the night, and I could only be held mildly responsible for the things spoken after midnight.

"Because I know there's more to you than meets the eye. Eventually, I'll prove that to everyone in town. I know deep down you're not who you say you are."

Despite his arrogance, he'd hit the proverbial nail on the head. While I really was Sadie Sabatini, there was no doubt that the current version of me made different choices than the past one. "Why are you calling? Just to harass me? I'm sure Chief Parker will be interested in knowing how you spend your time on the graveyard shift."

Something akin to a harrumph sounded over our connection. "Someone who is apparently very close to you has been arrested for assault. He's asking for you."

"Who is it?" I couldn't imagine who would use me as their one phone call. I was still relatively new here. The town would certainly have someone closer to them to serve as their point of contact.

"Either come down to the station and pay his bail, or I'm shipping him off to county for booking. I got better things to do than babysit your problem child."

"Fine. I'll be there as quickly as I can."

Twenty minutes later, I walked into the building representing the police presence in Wilson. It was a small structure with a stone exterior, lined with shrubs and flowering plants all along the front as landscaping. I stepped inside to be greeted by the smug face of Deputy Matthews. He reminded me a bit of Matthew McConaughey in looks only. His attitude and belief his "gut" was unerringly accurate had caused us to clash on more than one occasion. "Well, looky, looky, once again our resident bad girl has attracted the attention of the less desirable folk."

I did not have the patience for his condescending

tone at this time of the night or morning (depending on how you looked at it). I exhaled a long breath to keep from saying something that would result in me landing in the cell right next to the person responsible for making me their one phone call. "Are you going to let me see whoever this mystery person is, or are we going to play a game of cat and mouse the rest of the night?"

My comment made him crease his brows with a puzzled look. "What?"

Honestly, how did this man make it through the exams necessary to be employed as law enforcement? I started to explain, but he cut me off. "Oh, you mean bucking bronco and the clown." He chuckled again. "And I'm pretty sure you're the clown."

This man and his metaphors. He'd yet to get one right. "Can you please show me who you have so I can pay bail and resume my good night's sleep?" At this point, I'd settle for even a little rest before morning came calling.

He ignored my statement and gestured for me to follow him to the holding cell, which turned out to be nothing more than a locked room. When he opened the door, a blast from my past, in the very large shape of the man who served as the muscle on my former team, greeted me. "Dante?"

Dante nodded. He'd always been a man of action rather than words.

"So, the bad girl is reunited with the bad boy," Deputy Matthews laughed.

I ignored his comment, which wasn't hard since I

was trying to process why Dante was here, who he had assaulted, and what this meant for me. Thankfully, no one said anything more until the paperwork had been completed. Paperwork, which I noted, left off the name of the alleged victim. Was this Deputy Matthews intentionally keeping me in the dark? I wouldn't put it past him.

"All right, you're free to go, but you have a court appearance bright and early Monday morning in Crockett County. You best not leave town."

The short trip to my house was made in silence. I had no less than a million questions, but since he was the strong silent type, I wanted to wait until I could focus on his body language when he answered at least five or so of those million queries. Dante had retired from MMA fighting after being accused of doping. I'd proved he was set up by his fiercest rival. Instead of returning to the ring, he stayed with us and fought for our causes instead. Rarely had he chosen violence during our time together. His size alone was enough to dissuade most people from even looking like they were going to hurt us.

Once safely inside the privacy of my house, I gave him a big hug. "While I'm certainly happy to see you, what the heck is going on, Dante? Who did you assault? How did you find me?"

He returned my hug. "Missed you, too."

"Is that why you're here? You know why we had to split up. I'm sorry it had to be that way, but nothing has changed in that regard."

Sitting on my couch, he looked larger than life—at least, large enough to make me think there would only be room for one small person on the couch next to him. He struck an imposing contrast to the cream leather with his dark skin and hard as rock muscled frame. Dante shrugged. "We had nowhere else to go."

His choice of pronoun spiked my already high dose of adrenalin. "We who?"

He didn't say anything, merely arched one eyebrow.

Of course, I knew who the other person was that made up the *we* in his answer. "Natalie is with you?"

"She's around."

"How long have you two been together?"

"Since you left, and the team split." He'd uttered the phrase like it was the only logical conclusion.

"What have you been doing for the last year or so?"

"Small gigs, petty theft mostly." He smiled a bit. "You know Nat. Didn't wanna get dull. I was back-up."

The adrenaline left me in a whoosh and a pounding headache settled in its wake. "Why would you do that? We are supposed to be using our skills for good, not to rob people."

He shrugged. "We had to eat."

"That's BS and you know it. Each of you had enough money in your bank account to last you a lifetime. You didn't need to steal to eat."

Dante laughed. "All right, it was for the thrill."

My head shook as I tried to process what he'd

shared. "Why are you here? Where's Natalie? And, most importantly, who did you assault?"

He stood up and gave me another hug. "It's pretty simple, really."

"Well?" This whole scenario felt anything but simple to me.

"I beat the crap out of Miles Grant."

After a moment of allowing that statement to slide and then bounce around my sleep-deprived brain, I said the only thing I could think of. "You what?"

This time, there was no mirth, merely another shrug of his shoulders. "We've been following him. Nat never forgave him for making her gramps and gramma sick with those pesticides. We decided to make his life a living hell until he got out of the business completely."

At his statement, my anger dissipated. I stepped forward and laid my hand on his massive bicep. "If that's true, then I'll help you both prove it so we can be rid of him once and for all."

I looked up into those dark, obsidian eyes and read disbelief. Or, most likely, Natalie had convinced him I couldn't be trusted. She'd never forgiven me for not pursuing Miles to guarantee jail time or, perhaps, worse. Instead of agreeing to team up with me, he looked around. "You got a spare room I can crash in tonight?"

"Of course." I led him into the guest bedroom and showed him where everything was. I hadn't entertained any overnight guests yet, but one needed to always be prepared. Before I returned to my room, I made one more effort. "Dante, please tell me where Natalie is. I want to help you both."

He grabbed the towel and washcloth and stepped toward the bathroom. With a final look back, he offered a small smile. "You know how she is. You'll see her when she's ready."

With a nod, I left him to tend to his routine. Back in bed, the million questions I'd been lining up for Dante left the stage of my mind to allow for the million scenarios starting to run through my head. None of them ended well for me, Natalie, or Dante. Exhaustion finally won out, and my last thought was being grateful I owned my own business so I could choose what time I opened (or if I opened) each day. I wanted to talk more with Dante and formulate a plan to deal with Miles and try, once again, to set Dante and Natalie on the right path.

My alarm rudely went off at seven. I'd forgotten to turn it off. I pulled on my robe and went to check on Dante. Maybe he would want some pancakes for breakfast. I might even throw in some bacon since I went to bed without dinner last night.

My heart dropped into my stomach when I peeked in his room and found the bed made. A quick check around the house revealed what I already knew to be true. Dante was gone.

Chapter Three

I decided pancakes would still be a good idea. Dante was a grown man. I was no longer responsible for him. If he didn't show up in court on Monday, I'd lose the bail money, but it was a small price to pay. The pancakes were starting to bubble when my thoughts drifted to the look in his eyes last night. He no longer trusted me. After everything we'd been through, all the scrapes I'd gotten us out of–and, I admitted, that he'd gotten the team out of–the trust was gone.

Somehow, I needed to make it right. With or without Dante and Natalie, I'd prove Miles was still a bad actor and get him sent away for the rest of his life. The smell of batter burning returned my attention to what was supposed to be my breakfast. With more flourish than necessary, I dumped the half raw, half burnt pancakes in the trash and grabbed a Texas gold bar from my sweet stash. Tessa Tucker made the very best goodies this side of the Mason-Dixon line, which made supporting her business an easy choice.

With a cappuccino and gold bar in hand, I opened the back door and settled on my favorite chair to ease my mind with the reflection on Lake Amore. I'd enjoyed a couple sips when I heard knocking at the front door. Opening up the camera app on my phone to see who would dare intrude so early on a Saturday morning, my heart dropped. It was Deputy Matthews. Apparently, his shift wasn't over yet. Leaving everything on the table next to my lounger, I pulled my robe tighter around me and went to answer the door. "Can I help you?"

"Where is he?"

Even in my tired state, I knew who Deputy Matthews was asking about. I was also too tired to play games, so I offered honestly, "He's gone."

"I don't believe you. I'm coming inside."

He started to push past me, but I blocked his entrance. "Not without a search warrant, you're not."

Crimson crawled up his face as it flushed an angry red. "You're obstructing justice!" If he'd said it any louder, my neighbors would be treated to an early morning show.

Pausing a moment, I took a couple of deep breaths to ensure I remained civil. "How exactly am I doing that? I paid his bail and you said he needed to appear on Monday morning in court. What has changed in the last few hours to have you pounding on my door before eight on Saturday?"

His gaze darkened and he leaned closer to me. No longer yelling, his whispered tone frightened me more than if he'd been blustering about. "Because Miles Gentry was found murdered this morning outside his home."

Stunned, I stepped aside to allow him in for the search. I shouldn't have, but I knew with all certainty Dante wasn't here. The problem was, I had no idea what time he left. Less than ten minutes later, Deputy Matthews was standing in front of me. "Where did he go?"

"I honestly don't know. I showed him the spare bedroom and gave him a towel and washcloth and bid him goodnight. When I woke up this morning, he was gone."

"You need to come down to the station and make a statement."

"I've told you all I know. I'm happy to write it down, sign it, and drop it off later." The last thing I wanted to do was spend my day with a tired and grumpy deputy who, on his best day, irritated me. One look at him reinforced the notion this was shaping up to be a very bad day for him, and possibly me, too.

"I'm pretty sure it's not all you know. You had an altercation last night with Mr. Gentry."

I cut him off right there. "Before you get too carried away with your theories about my involvement in yet another case you don't want to actually try to solve, you should know his real name is not Miles Gentry."

"You know darn well it was."

I shook my head. "I know for certain it wasn't. Check his fingerprints. His real name is Miles Grant."

"And how do you know that?"

Ah, this was why making statements to the police on a sleep-deprived brain was never a good idea. "Our paths crossed when he worked for a large pharmaceutical company in California."

"You need to come down to the station. Chief Parker is gonna wanna talk to you." He no longer sounded angry, just tired. If he hadn't always been such a jerk to me, I might have felt sorry for him.

"Is Chief Parker even in the office yet?"

His face darkened. "He's at the crime scene. I came here to fetch our prime suspect."

He probably volunteered for this errand. I'm sure he had dreams about cuffing me—and not those kinds of dreams—so cuffing someone close to me was the next best thing. "I will call later this morning to confirm he's in the office. Once he is, I'll arrange to come in and answer his questions."

"Or you'll come with me now."

"Am I under arrest?"

"You know you're not," he growled.

"Then, we'll go with my plan. I hope you can go home and get some rest."

If looks could kill, they'd be calling the coroner right now. Thankfully, his glare didn't even make me feel sick. He was all bark and no bite. "See that you do, or the first thing I'm gonna do this evening is arrest you for obstruction of justice."

With that final warning, he stormed back to his truck. He waited to leave as Karen Bizzy was walking slowly down the sidewalk in front of my house. She waved him on, and he sped away. I could see her hesitation before she turned in my direction. "Well, hello, neighbor. What trouble are you in now?"

"None at all, Karen, but thanks for your concern." I swear, this woman always turned up at people's lowest moments. It was like she had a sixth sense or something. Though, in all fairness, she didn't appear to be her usual arrogant self. She looked as tired as I felt.

"I'm always concerned about Wilson's citizens. Be sure to come to the forum tomorrow night. I have interesting news to share about some of the candidates."

By interesting news, I'm sure she meant gossip or, better translated, something that would make the citizens of Wilson think twice about voting for whoever her latest victim was. She always had an agenda and, typically, it was to stir people into a frenzy to support her current cause. I waved, ready to end this conversation. I had real work to do. "Of course, I'll be there. Have a good day."

I stepped inside, not waiting for her response. I looked through the glass of my front door and saw her walking away. Something seemed off, but I didn't have time to investigate. I needed to find Dante and Natalie before the police did, then do my best to convince them to partner with me in their latest crusade. Though, with Miles dead, perhaps that chapter of their lives would be over and they could move on. Unfortunately, that thought brought me no joy as I was worried about the way the chapter ended.

My cappuccino had gone cold, so I made a new one and sat down to make a few notes for later. One habit I'd learned over the years was to write down everything I knew about a situation. Not only what I knew, but also assumptions and conclusions to the details that sometimes helped me piece together a picture of what had happened. And occasionally, depending on the situation, what needed to happen. There wasn't much to go on yet, but I might as well get started.

What had Dante and Natalie learned about Miles? Was there proof?

Need actual time of death and cause.

Are there any other potential suspects?

Though I'd made the suspect question the last on my list, it would probably move up in priority if Dante was arrested again. Normally, Jeremy would be my source for time and cause of death, but given how we left things last night, his willingness to bend rules on my behalf wasn't promising.

I'd barely ingested liquid caffeine when my phone buzzed. It was Emerson. *Lakeside Condos #13.*

That had to be the address for Miles. There was a good chance it was still buzzing with law enforcement. I would wait a bit before visiting the scene. *Thanks.*

It was terrible.

What was terrible?

He didn't answer, and an awful thought crossed

my mind. *Were you there this morning?* When I'd asked him to find his address, I didn't think he would stop by for a visit!

There was a long pause, even though I could see the three little dots indicating he'd started to type something. After an eternity, I texted again. *What did you see?? What happened!!* I hoped my use of double punctuation would convey the urgency in my request. Since I'd never witnessed him answering his phone unless it was his aunt, texting was my best option.

I sighed. This kid might have more natural curiosity than I did. Finally, a response came through. *Not now. Later. I have some things I have to do.*

Since I didn't have a choice, I responded, *Understood. Hope you're ok.*

The desire to call Jeremy to see what he knew made my fingers tremble from resisting the urge. He hesitated to share information when all was well between us. After last night, sadly, our relationship status was about as far away from positive as possible. Next on my source list was Kelsey. I was going to text her, but she was a morning person, so there was a good chance she was up. I pressed her number on my speed dial. After a few rings, I heard her cheery voice. "Hi, Sadie. How are you this morning? I heard about what happened last night."

Her information sources had to be legendary. "What exactly did you hear?"

"About you and Miles."

Oh, that piece of information had, no doubt, been

feeding the gossip mill from the moment it happened. "Yeah, not my finest hour."

She chuckled. "People will forget in no time."

News of a murder would probably trump my public altercation, even if it was with the victim. Ugh, eventually the police were going to ask me about that. I needed to learn what was traveling on the grapevine. "Anything else hot off the rumor line this morning?"

"No, why?"

How this detail had been kept private, I had no idea. One theory could be that the scene had been processed enough by the time the good folks of Wilson were on their way to work, the fitness center, or wherever they headed on a Saturday. It was also possible Kelsey had been celebrating with Pete last night more than she would admit, with at least a couple glasses of wine. As it was too early for fermented grapes, I offered, "Meet me for coffee in an hour and I'll fill you in."

"Okay. Want to meet at the Lakeside Grill and just bring our own? We can sit outside at a table by the lake."

This woman was brilliant. "I'll bring enough for both of us. Sound like a plan?"

"I never say no to your coffee. I'll bring the cups. See you then."

If last night and this morning hadn't drained the smile right out of me, her admission would have had me grinning from ear to ear. I did take a certain measure of pride in my ability to make the perfect cup.

Of course, the Italian coffee beans I'd carefully chosen didn't hurt, either. "See you then."

After making coffee and securing it in a thermos, I stepped outside. A slight shiver skittered across my skin. December in Texas was not cold by any means unless you'd lived here your whole life. In which case, you probably didn't really know the true meaning of cold. North Dakota, where I grew up, offered bone-chilling temperatures that stayed with you all winter and sometimes even into the spring. This was a piece of cake comparatively. I grabbed a jacket just in case and started out on a brisk walk.

About fifteen minutes and some beautiful scenery later, I'd arrived at my destination. Though you could technically see the lake from here, using the name Lakeside Condos might have been a stretch. The ugliness of the yellow and black police tape protecting the crime scene presented a stark contrast to the wooded area it surrounded. I'd arrived late enough that whatever crowd might have been here was long gone. With the incident happening outside, it was reasonable to assume Miles had known his attacker. Otherwise, why would he willingly come out in the middle of the night? Also, because other people lived here, it made me wonder if anyone had seen or heard anything. Even if the altercation occurred in the wooded area next to the condos, there should have been a struggle or voices loud enough to wake the residents, right? I know I would have been screaming if someone tried to kill me.

As I stood pondering, a voice interrupted my thoughts. "Good morning, Sadie."

I turned from the crime scene and saw Delaney Jeffries, one of the current board members, exiting the building. "Morning, Delaney. I didn't realize you lived here."

She nodded. "My home here in Wilson is currently undergoing renovations, so I did a short-term lease until they're finished." She smiled. "That's the beauty of working in IT, I can pretty much do my job from anywhere."

"Sure beats a one or two hour commute. Glad you were able to find a place close by. I'm sure with the elections coming up, even though your term isn't up, you'd want to be seen about the neighborhood."

"Never hurts." She grinned.

She joined me by the yellow crime tape. We were about the same height, but her hair was a reddish brown while mine was black as night. She took a drink from an insulated cup and adjusted her dark-rimmed glasses. Since she was here, I figured it couldn't hurt to ask. "Did you see or hear anything last night?"

Delaney shook her head. "Ironically, no. Though I can't understand how that is possible. Maybe if I'd heard something, I could have–"

"No, you can't think like that. Miles and his choices were not on you. Certainly, you're not responsible for whoever made the choice to end his life."

She sighed. "I know you're right, it's just so sad."

Though Miles was not a good man, she was right.

No one deserved to have their life ended for them. There were plenty of ways to pay for one's crimes, many of which he experienced. "You have any idea what happened?"

"Not really. The police knocked on my door around six this morning. Thankfully, I'd gotten up early to work on a project due Monday morning first thing." She finished her answer with a yawn.

"I'm sorry. That's never fun. Did they provide any clues or other information?"

She turned away from the scene, her chocolate eyes focused on me. "Why are you so interested in the events of last night? Did you know the man?"

"From a lifetime ago," I admitted. That's what it truly felt like, although my prior life kept intersecting with the new one I was trying to build here in Wilson.

Her intense gaze continued for another moment or two before she took a sip of her coffee. Finally, she answered. "They asked me if I heard any noises between the hours of four and five. It's reasonable to assume it was within that sixty-minute timeframe the incident occurred."

I had to admire her attention to detail. The fact she was also sharing information and providing at least an estimated time of death made me incredibly grateful. Though not as accurate as a coroner's report, it gave me a window to work with. "Very reasonable. Anything else?"

"Not really, sorry. I just feel bad for the boy."

"Which boy?" Worry spread like lightning through

my veins as I arrived at a reasonable guess what her answer would be.

"I think his name is Emerson."

This explained why he didn't want to share this over text. "What happened?" Maybe she could provide answers Emerson wouldn't...or couldn't.

Her expression morphed into one of sympathy. I was certain she could hear the fear in my voice as I asked. "He was the one who found the body."

Chapter Four

Oh, Emerson and I were going to have a chat about his not sharing the most important detail. I exhaled slowly. Despite how mature he tried to act, at the end of the day, he was a teenager, and barely one at that. How traumatizing! I would need to find him soon and do what I could to comfort and offer reassurance. "That must have been terrible for him."

She nodded. "He looked a little shaken up, but not as terrified as me if I stumbled across a dead body in the early hours of the morning." She shook her head. "What am I saying? I would be terrified to stumble across a body at any time of the day or night."

"Totally understandable." My support came out as a muttered response. All my thoughts were with Emerson now, willing him strength.

Her hand clasped my shoulder briefly and squeezed. Perhaps silently encouraging me for whatever challenges were ahead? "If I hear of anything else, I'll let you know."

"Thank you, ma'am. I appreciate it. And if you were up for re-election, you'd have my vote."

Her smile ticked up and she nodded. "Thank you, I appreciate that." She started to walk away but turned with a concerned look. "Be careful, Sadie."

"I will."

I returned my attention to the crime scene. Several of these wooded lots could be found around Wilson, which added to the "away from the city and burbs" vibe that attracted people to this little slice of heaven. They also provided a home to the ever-increasing deer population. Sadly, I feared eventually these havens for our animal population would be developed into housing or retail space. Inching closer, I peeked inside to see if anything (besides a deer) would jump out at me. There were a couple of patches where the under-growth appeared to be compressed as if something or someone had been sitting–or hiding–there. Of course, it could have been a deer or kids playing hide and seek. No way to tell.

There was also no way to tell if the police had finished their review of the crime scene or if they'd put the tape up to protect the area so they could do a more thorough search later. I was just about to leave when a glimpse of something yellow caught my eye. I glanced around and saw no one in the area. Ducking under the tape, I moved quickly and quietly to the object. Care-fully kneeling, I brushed some of the undergrowth away to find what didn't belong. There, in the pine needles and long grass, was a hard plastic item resembling a kid's ring. A flat circle over the hoop for your finger with a little spike on top. Maybe to hold something in place? What an odd thing to find here.

It could be a clue, or perhaps litter. Either way, I decided to take it with me. If it turned out later to be evidence, I'd tell Chief Parker I was just being a conscientious citizen and picking up the trash I'd seen. That was plausible (and partially true).

With nothing else to learn, I headed toward Lakeside Grill. One thought weighed heavier on me with each step I took. If Delaney was right about the time of the murder, that meant Dante could have left my house, made it here, and murdered Miles Grant.

* * *

The Lakeside Grill was situated along the shoreline of Lake Amore. Gentle waves lapped into rocks forming the border between the lake and the land. The restaurant had a few tables inside along with the bar, but typically patrons sat outside to enjoy the view. There was also seating on the concrete patio for those wanting service at the restaurant, and several picnic tables and cornhole games were spaced out among the grassy area surrounding the building. Next door was the main pool, surrounded by a fence. Except for winter when it might dare to be unseasonably cool, this was a popular hangout for residents of all ages.

I saw Kelsey sitting near the water, two cups on the table in front of her. "The big one is mine, right?" I teased as I sat down next to her.

She smiled, but I sensed concern lurking behind her light green eyes. "Today, I'm going to let you have the big one, but don't be surprised when I go for seconds."

"That seems reasonable." The coffee was poured, and we enjoyed the peace the lake brought.

After about ten minutes, Kelsey turned and looked at me. "So, what happened last night?"

Wanting to delay the inevitable, I kept my gaze on the water. "What happened where? There were several events over the last twelve hours. You'll need to narrow the timeline down for me."

The corner of her mouth quirking up could be seen in my peripheral vision. "That is certainly true. Let's start with the events at The Club."

An involuntary sigh escaped me. I might as well give her as much of the truth as possible. "Jeremy and I were having a nice time when I noticed someone seated nearby who looked familiar."

"And you couldn't resist?" There was a slight tease in her voice, but it was laced with enough seriousness for me to know she wasn't joking.

My head shook slowly. "No, I couldn't." I filled her in on the rest of the details, finishing with, "My goal was to make sure Mr. Cutter knew what kind of person he was associating with."

"How could you possibly know Miles? He just

moved in a few weeks ago. I've spent a little time with him. He was very charming and likeable."

I wanted to ask Kelsey about her time with Miles. Maybe that was what I saw in her expression. Perhaps he'd already used his wiles to trick her into believing his lies. Since I was reluctant to share too much about my time with him, I decided against it. She would eventually tell me. After a long pause, which I spent desperately trying to figure out a way to explain all of this without giving away too much, I answered. "Our paths crossed almost two years ago in California."

"Oh, I see. Were you working together?"

"You could say that." Technically, I was working against him, but one could reason we were in the situation together, even if he was an unwilling participant.

She shook her head and shot me a quick look of disapproval. "I did say that. I was wondering if you were going to further explain."

Deciding a half-truth was better than an outright lie, I opted for the version as close to the truth as possible. "I can't share the details of my assignment, but the team I was a part of discovered he was responsible for shady dealings that put people in harm's way along with skimming funds from his company."

"What kind of team was that?"

"I'm sorry, it's classified." As the details could endanger the other members of my crew, two of which were nearby, this was the best I could do on short notice. I hoped she would interpret this to be some type of government undercover situation as people often do when you toss out words like classified.

"I see." Her gaze returned to the lake.

Since she didn't say anything further, I decided to change the topic. "How well do you know James Cutter?"

She shrugged and continued to study the lake. "A little. He comes from money, and lots of it. After the family made their initial fortune, they turned their attention to more philanthropic endeavors. All their businesses in that arena fall under the "Cutter Cares" umbrella."

It felt like Kelsey knew more than a little about James and his family. "Catchy corporate motto, I suppose. Do you know anything about the relationship between James and Miles?"

"They were business partners."

I'd learned that from my brief interaction with the two men Friday night. I was curious if Kelsey knew more. "Any idea what kind of business?"

Abruptly, she stood up and started to pace in the area between the table and the lake. "Kelsey, what's wrong? I didn't mean to upset you."

She finally stopped and turned her attention back to me. " Miles was the big referral Pete and I were cele-brating last night."

"Oh."

She nodded, "Oh is right. His death will certainly complicate things, and most likely quash the deal. I don't know if James can carry on as the sole partner. From what I understood, Miles was the brains and James was the money."

"Were there other investors? Would any of them be able to keep things going?" I felt bad Pete and Kelsey were affected by this, too.

"I can't say for certain. Pete doesn't usually give details about his work, client confidentiality and all. I was surprised he shared as much as he did with me. I think he was hoping this deal would continue to grow and he might finally make partner at the law firm. He certainly alluded to that potential. He also inferred one investor planned on providing an additional infusion of cash about a month after the deal was first drawn up."

"No idea which one?"

Her bottom lip disappeared into her mouth as I waited for her answer. "I can only hazard a guess. Assuming Miles and James were the primary partners and had access to the Cutter fortune, I would imagine James would be making a sizable investment into their venture."

"That logic works for me absent, of course, of any additional factors to consider. Maybe all the other investors are loaded, too? Doesn't seem to be out of the ordinary around here." I offered a smile after my statement.

She returned to the picnic table, but this time she sat down across from me. "Agreed. Though, I'm not sure why there would need to be a delay. It's not like the Cutter family couldn't afford it."

"Maybe James was waiting to see more of Miles' business plan before he infused additional cash into the venture?"

"Maybe."

"Any idea when the month-long timeframe would be up, and the additional cash expected?"

She shook her head. "I can't be one hundred percent certain, but I would imagine sometime this coming week, give or take a couple days."

We both fell quiet, absorbed in our thoughts. I had no idea what Kelsey was thinking, but I tried to piece together the information she'd provided. If it was James, then why would he have to wait to invest more money? Miles couldn't have been happy with the delay unless it was the only option available. Kelsey indicated there might be other investors, but neither of us had any idea who. With Miles being in town only a few weeks, he couldn't have cultivated too many relationships at a level where people would invest large sums of cash, could he? I certainly wouldn't have given money to Miles, not that he even knew I was in town. "If the deal isn't dead, what might happen to it?"

She shrugged. "I assume all of his assets will go into probate and, once that's settled, they can decide if they want to continue the business venture."

"Any idea what the venture was going to be?"

Kelsey shook her head. "No, Pete didn't offer, and I didn't ask. Sorry."

"No worries. It's probably not important, anyway."

She offered a rueful smile. "Well, thankfully, other

than the nice dinner we had last night, it's not like I'd already ordered the curtains."

While I could normally speak Kelsey, her statement confused me. "What?" I laughed.

"An old saying from people who get paid on commission. Never order the curtains or make any large purchases until the commission is well in hand. You never know what might happen."

"Like one half of the business venture getting murdered even before it starts?"

"Yes, that definitely puts a fly in the ointment."

She was full of euphemisms today. "I'm sorry, my friend."

After a nod of acknowledgment, we fell into silence. She still seemed troubled. I put my hand across hers. "Everything else okay? Is something more going on besides the challenges with this deal?"

She clasped my hand. "I'll be fine. Just thinking about the past, wishing I would have done a few things differently."

"Want to talk about it?"

"No, not right now. We both have enough on our plates."

Thinking of all that had transpired in the last twenty-four hours or so, it was hard to disagree. "No argument here. You know I'm always available as a listening ear."

She nodded but didn't respond. After a few deep breaths, a smile returned to her face. "Everything's going to be all right. Let's change the subject."

Since thinking about Miles' murder and the fallout from it would keep a dark cloud over both of us, she was probably right. "Okay, I'm game for a topic turn. What would you like to talk about?"

"Have you decided who you're going to vote for yet?"

I laughed. "The candidate forum isn't until tomorrow night. I'd like to hear what they have to say before making my final decision."

"I understand, but you have to be leaning toward or away from someone."

"Definitely not Karen. No matter what she says, I'm not putting that Bizzy-body in any position that gives her more power than she already has."

Kelsey laughed, and it lightened the dark mood brewing since we first started talking. "I totally agree with you on that one. Besides, I'm pretty sure Estelle will be running a behind-the-scenes campaign against her, so chances of victory are slim."

Estelle, also known as EZ, had recently become a property owner in Wilson, much to Karen's disappointment. She'd earned the nickname because of her chosen line of work, but she also happened to be very close to the Birmingham family, especially the patriarch, Robert Birmingham. Though no one ever said anything, everyone in town seemed to understand whatever their relationship was, it was off-limits as a topic of conversation or gossip. And no one wanted to upset the Birmingham family tree. "You have a valid point. I'm leaning toward Tessa Tucker for one of my three votes. She has a locally owned business, supports the community, and I think a younger viewpoint might help Wilson be better prepared for the future."

Kelsey raised her coffee cup. "Here, here. Well said. I would drink to that toast, but I'm pretty sure it's gone cold."

"You want a refill of the hot stuff?"

"No, thank you. I best be getting home to Pete. He always makes a late brunch on Saturday, the one and only day he steps foot in the kitchen. I don't want to miss out on that."

"I would never ask you to make such a sacrifice. I'll see you tomorrow night at the forum."

She nodded and got up from the table. I followed suit. After a quick hug, she hesitated as though she was weighing her next words. "I hope someday you'll trust me with the truth about your past life, whatever it is." Before I could say anything, she continued. "Until then, I'll respect your desire for privacy as I'm sure you have a good reason."

Moisture gathered in my eyes at her kind words. I pulled her into a hug again and whispered, "I hope someday I can as well. Until then, I'm very grateful for your friendship and your patience with me."

Once released, she offered a small smile and nod before walking away. I decided to enjoy the lake for a few more minutes before going home. There was nothing there, anyway, besides an empty house and more questions.

Thoughts of Emerson surfaced. I worried how he was handling everything. I also didn't want him to feel pressured. I sent a quick text. *If you want to talk, I'm here. Anytime, day or night.*

After several minutes of no reply, I decided I'd check in with his Aunt Isabella a little later to make sure he was okay. My phone buzzed with an incoming call. At first, I thought it might be Emerson, but my heart skipped a beat when the caller ID revealed it was Jeremy. I took a deep breath and exhaled slowly, willing myself into a sense of calm. "Hello?"

"Sadie, what in the good Lord's name is going on?"

I wasn't sure I appreciated his tone and, just as I'd mentioned to Kelsey, a lot had been *going on* in the last twenty-four hours, so he would need to clarify. "I beg your pardon?"

"My buddy over at the county sheriff's office recognized your name on some paperwork for a bail bond from last night. What are you doing bailing someone out of jail in the middle of the night? Who was this person to you?"

Obviously, his buddy hadn't updated him on the whole Miles murder development. He wasn't going to get that information from me. Not today. "I'm not sure if I should be flattered or annoyed by your jealousy. You've made it very clear we can only be friends, so regardless of what he might be to me, I'm not sure how this is any of your business." I know, it was very petty, but this man had a way of pushing all my buttons.

Normally, it was the good ones he pushed, but sometimes... That detail, compounded by my lack of sleep, meant he was in for the sassy side of Sadie if he kept it up.

There was a long pause. Finally, I heard a long exhale come through the phone. "I'm not jealous. I'm worried."

"I appreciate that, but I'm fine."

"I'm sure you are," he scoffed.

More time elapsed, allowing dread to build in my stomach with each passing second. Finally, I couldn't take it anymore. "Now that we've established I'm fine, was there anything else?"

"I'm sure you know Miles Gentry, formerly known as Miles Grant, was murdered last night."

Okay, so maybe his buddy at the sheriff's office *was* keeping him in the loop. "I'm aware."

"Anything I should know?"

I hated that I couldn't be certain if he was asking out of concern for my wellbeing or to share information with his buddy as repayment for the tip about little ol' me. Either way, I was all out of sharing for the morning. "Sounds like you know as much or more than me."

"So, you knew when you saw him last night he had changed his name?"

"Yes." No sense in lying about that.

After more silence, I was just about to tell him I had to go when he offered, "I'm sorry about last night. I know you're upset with me, and I understand. I assume you know why I'm upset as well?"

"Mm hmm." Again, no sense in denying it. We'd had the same circular and non-productive discussion multiple times in the few months we'd been "non-dating."

"Will you still take my calls?"

Part of me wanted to smile since I'd asked him that question multiple times after we'd had a disagreement or when he was aggravated by choices I'd made. It would be wrong to reply any differently than he'd always answered me. "Of course. And Jeremy?"

"Yes?"

"It was just an old friend passing through town who got himself into a little trouble. Nothing more."

"Are you in trouble?"

"Not at the moment." The corner of my mouth ticked up as I imagined the look crossing his face at my answer.

"Okay, I'll let you go, then. Please be careful. And Sadie?"

"Yes."

"Please call if you need to."

I didn't want to promise I would because, depending on the situation, whatever I wanted or needed might send our relationship down a much more difficult road than the one we currently travelled, which had plenty of potholes on its own. Instead, I simply offered, "I appreciate you. Thanks."

We said our goodbyes and I hung up. My feelings were all jumbled. The lack of proper rest and the collision of my past with my present only added to my exhaustion. I started the walk home. Maybe a nap would help.

I'd barely made it in the door when a video call came through. It was my parents. We usually spoke once a week on Sunday evenings. A look at my watch confirmed it was only a little past noon on Saturday. I worried something was wrong. Forcing a smile on my face, I accepted the call. "Ciao, Mamma and Papà."

"Ciao, bella. How are you today?" My father's deep, cheerful voice pushed all the negative emotions to the back of my brain to be brought out to deal with later.

"I'll be better once I know why you're calling outside our normal schedule." I quickly added, "Of course, I'm always happy to hear from you any time. Are you both all right?"

Before my father could answer, my mother grabbed the phone and gushed, "We're wonderful! We just heard from your sister. She got the job with the PR firm she was hoping for."

At least that explained the early call. My parents took extreme pride in their daughters. "That's great news! What will she be doing at the new company?"

My mother laughed. "I can tell you her title and how she explained it to me." She shrugged. "I under-stand exactly what she does about as much as I under-stand whatever it is that you've been doing the past several years of your life. It doesn't really matter to me, though. I'm proud of you both."

My mother was a registered nurse and had devoted her entire career to helping those less fortunate without easy access to healthcare. From working as a nurse at Doctors Without Borders, where she met my father, to her untiring work at VA hospitals, her kind and compassionate nature had healed both bodies and souls over the years. I smiled. "Thank you, Mamma. We can only hope to do half as much good as you have."

With a blush at my compliment, she waved it away. "Here, I'll let your father explain."

She handed the phone to my dad. He was smiling, too. The love he held for my mother was one for the storybooks. Maybe that's why my sister and I had never settled down–we were looking for someone who would love us with the same devotion our father loved our mother. Did those men even still exist? "Your sister's official title is publicist. She explained her role is to manage the public image of the company she works for."

My mother came into view again. "Sounds like a fixer to me."

I chuckled. "Mamma, that can mean a lot of different things depending on the context. Probably best not to use that term." Ironically, her new job sounded a little like what I'd done for the past ten years–fixing things the justice system had gotten wrong.

My father smiled. "Yes, but in this instance, when corporations bungle and make themselves look bad to the public, she helps 'fix' the situation and sets them on the right path again."

"She is well suited to that type of role." I kept my concern quiet regarding what might be required of her. I'd witnessed some questionable tactics by other people in similar professions over the years. I prayed my sister didn't have to resort to such means to be successful.

"I'm confident in her abilities. Both of my daughters are very business savvy. Speaking of that, how's Tesoro doing now that you've been in business for two quarters?"

My father was big into business. He'd worked in several areas of finance and currently served as an investment advisor at Berkshire Hathaway in Nebraska. "We've been steadily increasing monthly sales and word is spreading throughout not only the community of Wilson but into Crockett County, too."

"That is wonderful news. Before long, the good people of Houston will be making the hour or so drive to check out your shop."

"From your lips to God's ears, Papà." Seeing their smiling faces made me miss them even more. "When are you coming for a visit?"

My mother grabbed the phone back. "We want to come soon, but you know your father has to wait for the end of everything."

I laughed. "Yes, I know. Month-end, quarter-end, and year-end. So, January, maybe? Coming to Texas then will be warmer than Nebraska!"

"Very true. We will discuss and make some plans.

Until then, you take care of yourself and we'll talk next week?"

"Of course, Mamma." A quick thought slid to the front of my mind. "May I speak to Papà again for a moment?"

"Yes, my beautiful girl. I love you."

"I love you, too." Despite having turned thirty on my last birthday, I still enjoyed when she used that term of endearment.

When my father's face came back into view, his brows were furrowed and his lips were pressed in a thin line. "What is it, Sadie?"

"Nothing to worry about." I smiled to put him at ease. "I met a man who was an investor last night. I'm just curious if you know anything about the family who operates under the 'Cutter Cares' umbrella."

"If you're looking for investors, my offer still stands."

My heart warmed at his statement. "I know, Papà, but truly, I'm doing all right at the shop. Besides, isn't it you who tells me to make sure my expenses help offset my income before taxes are due? I'm watching my books very closely, just as you taught me."

He nodded. "You are going to be very successful, of that I have no doubt. I will see what I can learn and email you."

"Thank you. I love you."

"I love you, too."

After the call, I wandered into the kitchen for something to eat. I pulled the makings of a salad out of the fridge, grabbed my cutting board, and went to get my favorite knife. It wasn't in the block where it should be. I checked the dishwasher, even though I typically hand-washed them. Not there, either. Maybe I had taken it to a community potluck or something and forgot to bring it home. This was stacking up to be a real banner day. I could use another knife, but my desire for a salad had fled. Returning the vegetables to the fridge, I pulled out some leftovers and heated them up.

With my make-do lunch, a pad of paper, and a pen, I headed out to the deck. Might as well enjoy the sunshine while it was here. I grabbed the paper I'd started making notes on, gathered my thoughts, and started to write.

Miles changed his last name and convinced James Cutter to invest in a new business.

James made an initial investment. Possibly other investors as well. Potential that one of the investors (most likely James?) was going to invest about a month after the deal was drawn up. No idea why.

Time of death estimated between 4 and 5 a.m. Saturday morning.

Miles likely knew his attacker.

Dante left my home sometime in the middle of the night.

Odd piece of yellow plastic found in the wooded area where the murder occurred.

After a few more moments, my hand trembled as I wrote down one more item:

Natalie had made it her mission to make Miles' life difficult.

I tossed the pen and paper onto the table next to my lounge chair. Was Natalie capable of murder? Or, equally disturbing, had she somehow convinced Dante to do it for her?

Chapter Five

Sunday morning came entirely too early. Between the events of Friday and Saturday, peaceful sleep had eluded me for the most part. Thanks to the work ethic my parents instilled in me, I knew I still needed to go into Tesoro. Inventory had to be finished, and I wanted to make sure everything was set for Monday.

I arrived at the store a little after nine. I made good progress and busied myself arranging new pieces of jewelry. Sales indicated these items were very popular for the ladies in Wilson. A knock on the door surprised me.

Someone apparently doesn't understand the meaning of the word closed. Such sassy thoughts meant more caffeine was required to get through the day without hurting anyone. At the door was Denise McDowell, standing there in her Sunday finest. Platinum blonde hair, which normally hung just above her shoulders, had been swept into a simple up-do that, I noted with pride, showed off a beautiful pair of earrings she'd purchased from my shop. The makeup around her eyes intensified their dark blue color and her lips, painted red and glossed, were framed in a smile. "Good afternoon, Sadie. Can I come in?"

Not having one reason to deny her request, and since the fact the store was closed didn't seem to deter her, I let her in. "Hi, Denise. Is everything okay?"

She smoothed imaginary wrinkles from her skirt before a sly smile appeared. "I'm here to browse and learn things."

A sigh and eye roll begged to be let out to play, but I kept my face impassive as I moved to sit behind the counter. "Learn things about what?"

She took a few sashaying steps in the direction of the jewelry counter. Without even looking at me, she asked, "Like who you are planning to vote for."

Because three seats were open, each property owner had one vote for each. I already planned on giving Tessa one, but I decided to learn more about Denise's intentions. "First, share with me why you're running. From what I've learned, you typically stay away from local politics. Why now?"

She shrugged. "Why not now?"

I didn't answer what I assumed was a rhetorical question. The arch of my eyebrows and tilt of my head hopefully indicated I was still waiting for a real answer.

Denise laughed. With a wave of her hands, she huffed. "All right, you win. At first, I admit it was just to be near that hottie, Alan Knightly."

When Denise and I first became friends, she had a lot of fun describing Alan to me. Her fascination with him was no big secret to anyone who lived in Wilson. "You said at first. What changed your mind?"

"With all the changes in the powers that be recently in the ladies' association, I've assumed responsibility for a lot of the projects they've got going on. I confess, I like them looking to me somewhat as a leader. I've never had that kind of respect before." She shrugged. "So, I want to be in a position to make sure people are listening to what we have to say."

To her credit, she sounded sincere. Maybe the choice to give her one of my votes would be a sound decision. "That seems like a much better reason. I promise to give the matter serious consideration."

Her smile returned in full force. "Hey, that's all a gal can ask. I'll see you tonight!"

"See you tonight."

The door had barely closed on her departure when a soft thump followed by a shuffling sound came from the back room. I quickly locked the door and double checked the closed sign. Hopefully, everyone else would take the hint and come back tomorrow. If it was a burglar, I didn't want any innocent bystanders getting hurt. Though robbing someone in broad daylight felt unlikely, one could never be too careful. I knew in my heart of hearts who had caused the noise, though.

Stepping into the back room, my hunch was confirmed. I leaned against the door jamb and crossed my arms. "Nice of you to finally show yourself, Nat.

You here to say hello or, given the fact you're sitting in front of my safe, here to rob me?"

Natalie continued to work the dial, her ear pressed against the door. A moment later, the safe opened. With a toss of her ponytail and a triumphant smile, she gracefully rose from her seated position. Her long, willowy frame gave her the ability to fit in places others would not. Add to that her legendary flexibility from years training as a gymnast and she was the ideal candidate for a world class thief. "If I'd truly wanted to rob you, I would have simply done this at night. Though, I admit I didn't expect you here on a Sunday."

"So, you were planning to rob me."

She laughed. "Well, yeah. But I was going to return it to you after you panicked a bit. Just trying to teach you a lesson after all those you taught me."

"Did any of those lessons sink in?" I was pretty sure they hadn't since she'd followed Miles across the country to exact revenge. I couldn't remember that being a part of any lesson.

"Really, Sadie, your security measures are seriously lacking. Did you learn nothing during our time together?"

I noticed she didn't answer my question, but I decided to let it slide for now. "Well, not everyone is as gifted a thief as you are. Most people around here would have a difficult time getting through the window, much less cracking a safe."

"True, but if you really want to protect your little

trinkets, you may want to step up your security measures."

As Natalie *was* a gifted thief, I opted to not share that there were motion sensors hidden all over the store as well as pressure plates on the windows and doors that would alert me to any potential intruders. Of course, those measures were turned off when I was here. "I'll keep that in mind. Thanks for the check on my security. Now that you've proven your point, want to close my safe up?"

Her genuine laughter made my heart hurt a little for the relationship we used to have. From what Dante had shared, I suspected our closeness was in the past. "There. Safe as expensive bugs in a rug. Probably should change the combination now."

I didn't respond to her statement, though I would make sure the change was made. Instead, I asked, "Where's Dante? The police want him for questioning."

She crossed her arms and huffed, "He didn't kill anyone!"

"Did you?" The guilt at having to ask the question came as quickly as the words left my mouth. I hadn't even been able to look her in the eyes.

"How can you even think that?"

The sound of hurt in her question forced me to meet her gaze. "I'm sorry, but I had to ask. Dante told me about your little escapades to make Miles' life a living hell. Revenge blinds us. You hated Miles for what he did to your parents and grandparents, so you stalked him and harassed him. It's not a big leap to believe you might have taken the final vengeful step and killed him."

At my words, she reached into the small cross-body bag hanging near her hip and pulled out a wrapped candy. Opening it, she slid it onto her finger and put the large candy diamond in her mouth. I'd forgotten she was a self-soother. Instead of thumb sucking, as I'm sure she did as a child, she'd exchanged her thumb for the old school ring pop candy.

It only took me a moment to make the connection. The piece of plastic I'd found in the woods had to be what was left of one of those when the candy was gone. I'm certain the horror and shock echoing throughout my body showed on my face. "Natalie Dawson, you were there!"

"Where?"

"In the wooded area where Miles' body was found. You left the remains of your ring pop behind. You're worried about the security of my store, yet you left incriminating evidence at the crime scene. Lucky for you, I found and removed it before the police had time to properly search for clues. How could you be so careless? I *know* I taught you better than that."

She darted from the safe to my position faster than a lioness pounced on her prey. With a sweep of one leg, she knocked me from my standing position to flat on my back. Immediately, she straddled my body and fixed a glare on me, the intensity of which I don't think I'd ever seen from her before. "I admit to stalking him, maybe even waiting outside his condo to follow him, but I did not kill him. After all the time we spent together, how could you even think I was capable of murder?"

It took a few moments to catch my breath after my abrupt meeting with the floor. While recovering, I studied her face, which wasn't hard given it was close enough to feel every hot exhale of her breath. Wanting to give myself a little more time to read her, I offered a half smile. "I see Dante has been teaching you a thing or two since we parted ways."

She merely stared, so I continued. "If your position is that neither you nor Dante killed Miles, at least tell me why Dante beat him up so badly the night before. And why did he call me to get him out? I know both of you had the means to pay. You could have posted bail and skipped town, never to be seen again."

The hurt in her expression morphed into something that frightened me. I might not have known all the emotions darting around in her gaze, but I'd seen enough hatred in my years on this earth to recognize it in Natalie's dark green eyes. Her laugh sounded hollow as she stood and towered over me. "Because I learned from the best."

With those words, she returned to the window she'd arrived through and, with an ease that defied explanation, lifted her body through the opening. Once outside, she leaned through the window. "I'll never forget you betrayed me. See you later, Sadie."

On that haunting note, she was gone.

Her parting words left me shaken to my very core. Even though Dante had shared similar information, he hadn't delivered it with the same malevolence as Natalie. I truly didn't want to believe either of them were capable of murder, but this whole situation gave me serious pause.

I busied myself for the next hour or so watching the YouTube videos necessary to teach myself how to change the combination of my safe. I wouldn't put it past Nat to break in again and take something, just to prove her point. While she could certainly crack the safe again, I wasn't going to make it easy on her.

After that, I couldn't concentrate, couldn't sit still, and couldn't be productive. Just when I'd decided to go home and give myself a late afternoon kayak ride to help dispel nervous energy, there was a knock on the door. At this rate, maybe I would begin opening on Sunday afternoons. Once church was over, people might be inclined to stop in and do a little shopping. I closed the safe and walked to the front. Opening it, I smiled. "EZ, so nice to see you. What brings you here today?"

She shrugged. "I saw your truck parked out front and wondered what you were doing here on a Sunday. Everything all right?"

Estelle Zimmerman and I had fought hard to become friends. And, by that, I mean literally fought. Thanks to a mutual enemy, we formed an alliance and, somehow, it had stuck. This was the first time, however, she'd made it into my store. I knew her well enough to know if I said anything about her being thoughtful to check on me, she'd flip me off and leave. Instead, I offered a smile of gratitude. "All is well with the store. Finishing up inventory and getting everything ready for opening tomorrow." I noticed her looking around a bit at some of the new displays of jewelry I'd just set up. "Anything catch your eye?"

She nodded. "Okay if I look around since I'm here?"

"Of course."

As she made her way over to take a closer look, I took the opportunity to study her. For a woman who had to be in her early sixties, she looked much younger and was in exceptional shape. It made me wonder if she'd been blessed with a good metabolism or, because of her chosen occupation, she'd worked hard to keep her body in primetime proportions. She was a fan favorite at an establishment on the outskirts of town called The Foxy Lady. She'd quickly taught me the error of underestimating her, a lesson I wouldn't soon forget. She studied the pieces for several minutes before pointing to a pair of earrings. "I'd like a closer look at these."

I opened the case and pulled out her selection. "These starfish are made of Murano glass. They use the turquoise and metallic colors, then carefully craft it into the desired shape around a handmade bead. Because of the process, no two pairs are alike."

She held them up to her ear and looked in the mirror on top of the jewelry case. "They're beautiful. I know you aren't officially open, but I can pay with cash."

How could I say no to that? "Of course. Come on over to the counter and I'll write up the receipt."

As I worked on completing the transaction, I decided to make small talk. "Are you going to be at the candidate forum tonight?"

EZ smiled. "I wouldn't miss it for the world."

"Really?"

She crossed her arms, tilted her head down, and frowned. "Why, because someone like me wouldn't be interested in local politics?"

Realizing she misunderstood my intention, I clarified. "No, not at all. It's just that most people don't care much about these races. To be honest, I wouldn't be going if Kelsey hadn't worn me down and made me pinky swear I'd be there."

Her gravelly laughter brightened the dark mood hovering over me since Nat's visit. Years of smoking cigarettes probably added to the deepness of the rich sound, but it was uniquely her. It made it easier to find her in a crowd. Of course, you could also find her by locating the largest congregation of men, but that was beside the point. "I plan to be there to make sure Ms. Karen Bizzy-body doesn't get away with anything and to make sure she doesn't get elected."

I nodded as I handed her the receipt and her new earrings. "I'm right there with you. The last thing that woman needs is any real power. She causes enough havoc on our town as it is."

Immediately, she took off the earrings she wore and put on the new ones. "How do I look?"

"Amazing, as always. They accent your cheekbones and are a good compliment to your blonde hair."

"Even when they're in ponytails?"

I laughed. "Even then."

"Good, 'cause you know how much I like my ponytails."

Since that's the only way I'd ever seen her wear her hair, it was a safe guess. "I do."

"Gotta give the boys whatever fuels their fantasies, you know." The smirk on her face was priceless.

Not really, but I decided to play along. She had, after all, just paid cash for an expensive pair of earrings from me. "I have no doubts you're adept at learning and giving them whatever they want."

EZ laughed. "Well not *everything*."

"Touché."

"See you tonight, Sadie."

"See you, EZ. Thanks for stopping by."

"You've got good stuff in here. I'll be back again, promise. May even bring you some more business once the other girls see these earrings."

"That would be great. Thank you!" And I meant it. I didn't care who my customers were, as long as they were paying.

* * *

A few hours later, I was in the downstairs area of The Club seated amongst sixty or so of Wilson's residents. This was my first opportunity to witness the election process for the board of our Community Improvement Association or CIA, which was a fun acronym when you thought about it. I turned toward Kelsey as I witnessed the sheer number of bodies still making their way into the large room. "Are there usually this many people at a Meet the Candidates event?" While I loved America, when it came to those who governed our nation or my community, there was a lot of room for improvement, if you asked me. Which, ironically, no one did.

Kelsey shook her head in response to my question. "No, this is an unprecedented election with three open seats. It's a big year in local politics. Depending on who gets elected, there could be a shift of power in the community. Because some believe new leadership is needed and there are others who like things the way they are, this is the hottest news in Wilson since..." She turned to me and offered a quirky grin. "Well, since you came to town."

"Very funny, very funny." I elbowed her gently for good measure. Though, in all fairness, my arrival and subsequent events did cause quite a stir. Part of which was the reason for one of the empty board positions.

A few minutes later, the crowd quieted as the local patriarch of Wilson, longest tenured member of the board, and reigning president, Robert Birmingham, came to stand behind the podium. His posture and poise sent signals of power, and it was easy to see why people looked to him for direction. I put him around six feet tall with a solid build. Not muscled enough to make me think he spent a lot of time in the gym, but fit enough to know he took good care of himself. Though too seasoned for my tastes, with his wealth, Southern charm, and classic good looks, it wasn't hard to see why people were drawn to him (including EZ).

He cleared his throat and smiled as he began to speak. "Good people of Wilson, thank you for coming out this evening. I'm grateful you understand the importance of this election and choosing the right folks to fill these empty seats. As you know, both Ms. Jeffries and I are not up for re-election." He gestured to Delaney sitting to his right. I noted she appeared a little ill-at-ease being the center of attention. She adjusted her glasses, a nervous tendency people sometimes displayed, and smiled at the crowd.

Robert continued, introducing the other current board members. "Please welcome Alan Knightly, whose seat is up for re-election."

As Alan stepped into the room to take his seat, he was met with applause, along with some throat clearing sounds and a few dramatic sighs. I did a quick survey of the room. Alan had a small fan base, but he had his work cut out for him if he was going to keep his seat.

Robert did nothing to quiet the crowd's displeasure. It was no secret the Knightly and Birmingham family were embroiled in a longstanding feud that rivaled the Hatfields and McCoys. The corner of his mustached lip might have even curled in a slight smirk. Or maybe I imagined that. The Birminghams weren't exactly fans of mine. The feeling was mutual.

"And, of course, each of you are familiar with JB Nester." A round of applause from the back caused the middle-aged man with a slightly rounded mid-section to raise his hand in greeting and nod to his cheering brigade in the standing room only section.

"Looks like Jim Bob has a fan club," I leaned and whispered to Kelsey. This time, she graced me with a gentle elbow. Before the night was over, we both might have sore ribs to talk about over a bottle of wine. "Shhh," she reprimanded, but I caught the grin on her face. She tried to be all proper and behave, but I knew it was mostly an act.

The introductions continued. "Please join me in welcoming the remaining candidates who have not served on the board in the last term. Tessa Tucker..."

When her name was announced, her cheering section—a.k.a me—clapped with enthusiasm. "Go Tessa!" I offered in a voice that filled the room, garnering curious looks from the audience, a glare from Robert, and another elbow from Kelsey. Tessa just smiled and appeared to be holding back laughter.

Robert ignored my outburst and continued. "Karen Bizzy..." As Karen took her seat, no one cheered. "Denise MacDowell...and Jackie Price." Those two ladies were greeted with a respectable amount of positive vibes from the crowd.

With introductions completed, Robert continued.

"Before the candidates give their statements, I'd like to offer a moment of silence for our final candidate, a gentleman whose cruel and untimely death ended his campaign for a life in Wilson."

Everyone around me took off their hats and bowed their heads in respect. I wasn't wearing a hat, but no way was I bowing my head in deference to a man who had caused so many people harm. Robert noticed me and shot a disapproving glare. I crossed my arms and returned his stare. Once he realized I wasn't going to bend to his will, he coughed and said, "Thank you, everyone. Let's begin with Alan Knightly."

Alan stood and moved to stand behind the podium. In true Robert fashion, he delayed taking a few steps aside to have a quick stand-off. Both men were of similar height. Alan's salt and pepper hair, mostly still pepper, was a stark contrast to Robert's snowy white pate. Their eyes shot angry lasers at each other just long enough to make their point. Robert didn't want to be perceived as a jerk, he was just trying to establish dominance in a game I doubted few truly cared about.

Once alone, Alan offered a gratuitous smile in Robert's direction. "Thank you, Mr. Birmingham." He then returned his gaze to us. It was nice to know that even with an age-old feud raging, everyone could still play nice in the proverbial sand box. "And thank you, good citizens of Wilson. I'm asking for your vote this year to support the fight for progress in Wilson and all the wonderful things Texas stands for. While some—"

He cast a sideways glance in Robert's direction, "– would keep us stuck in the ways of the past..."

Apparently, a tickle crawled down Robert's throat about that time, making him cough a sound that resembled the brown piles left behind cattle that roamed the open pastures around here (for those who aren't from around these parts, it rhymed with 'full-knit' or 'school sit'). Despite the disrespect it showed, the mighty Robert Birmingham acting like a schoolyard bully brought a smile to my face. It was so beneath him, yet he couldn't resist. While most kept quiet, I swear I heard the distinctive sound of EZ's chuckle. She was probably on retainer to laugh at Robert's behavior whenever he was trying to be funny.

Alan gave him the ol' side-eye, but he continued. "Tonight, I want to remind you that a vote for me is a vote for moving forward into a new era, while still protecting all the things that make Texas great and Wilson the wonderful place we've chosen to live. Thank you."

The applause was reasonable as he took his seat. JB Nester was up next. His steps to the podium were slow and measured. Though I was no doctor, he looked ill. He cast a quick glance at Robert, and then one at Alan, before leaning forward to the microphone. "Thank you, everyone, for your years of support. I am grateful to serve and hope to continue to do so in the future."

I cut a look at Kelsey, who shrugged. If she didn't know, I would wager no one did. He appeared fine when they first came out. What happened in the ten or fifteen minutes before it was his turn to speak?

Denise stood up next and smiled at the crowd. "Well, I guess if that's all he has to say, I'll use my time and the rest of his."

Her posse laughed and clapped politely. She nodded her thanks in their direction. "I agree that change is good, but both Alan and I know not all change is. Take, for example, our buddy Jim Bob here. Did you know that he works for a company that is secretly trying to replace oil and gas as our main energy source?"

Collective gasps from the audience arose followed by murmurs. JB's complexion took on an even greener hue. Denise continued. "Wilson was founded on oil and gas. And to add flames to the fire of destruction on our way of life, not only is Jim Bob here supporting development that will harm the economic landscape, one of my other opponents, Karen Bizzy, along with her elitist attitude, seeks to keep Wilson from being inclusive of all the wonderful folks who live on our little peninsula."

"Damn straight!" EZ's voice rang out above the continued murmurs resulting from Denise's words.

Robert shot her a look, but I wasn't sure if it was reproach or respect. He turned his attention back to Denise. "Please wrap it up, Ms. McDowell."

Denise offered her sassiest of smiles (and I knew this because I'd seen it before). "Of course, Mr. President." She turned to the audience, now gaping in surprise at all the things she revealed. "So, we have JB trying to change our way of life, and KB–that's Karen Bizzy, if y'all weren't tracking with me–has already made our lives difficult with the little power she already has. I mean, really, all those nonsensical violations of alleged deed restrictions, extending no grace for even the smallest of infractions. Is that really the kind of environment we want to support?"

Not surprisingly, Karen stood at this accusation. "Why you little, good for nothing hussy. I ought to go back through all my records to prove the number of times I *didn't* write someone up. I mean, let's be honest, do we want anarchy and a lack of order to rule our society? I think not! I aim to bring honor to our little community and a place everyone can be proud to invite their friends and family. Instead of worrying about where your next roll in the hay is going to come from, DM, maybe you should–"

Before Karen could finish that thought, her smartwatch lighting up repeatedly caught her attention. She stopped the tirade long enough to read the alert on her phone. She looked at everyone. "Please excuse me for a moment."

She reached into her purse and pulled out her phone. After a moment, her demeanor did a one-eighty faster than a cowboy could get kicked off a broncin' bull. She looked to Robert, who was studying her with curiosity. Probably because none of us had ever seen her this contrite. "My apologies, Mr. President. I would like to announce that, due to personal reasons, I'm withdrawing from the race and giving my support to Jackie Price."

Another gasp rippled through the crowd. What in the name of bluebells in Texas was going on? Kelsey's elbow and subsequent nod directed my attention to the look of surprise on Jackie's face. "She must know something. I don't know how Karen feels about Jackie, but I'm pretty sure she *hates* Jackie's brother, Lester." I whispered at a level I trusted only she could hear.

Kelsey nodded. "Agreed. Any idea why Karen is sending a look of pure hatred this way?"

I turned in my seat enough to see who was sitting behind us. There were a lot of people, of course. I recognized many faces but didn't know their names. Lester was there, which could explain the fury. I also noticed EZ was in the area as well. I remembered EZ's words from earlier today about ensuring Karen didn't get elected. Her response to the announcement could be categorized as satisfaction. Had she somehow masterminded whatever Karen had seen? What *was* in that message? It had to be something significant for Karen to do such an about face in front of a large audience. But if EZ was behind it, why would she have Karen lend support to Jackie? I didn't think EZ was a big fan of the Price family, either, but she was always full of surprises. I made a mental note to try to ask around about that later.

Robert banged the gavel. "Order, I say. Order!"

The crowd quieted, and Karen took her leave.

Robert cleared his throat. "All right, Ms. Price, would you like to speak next?"

Jackie was marginally better looking than her brother. He resembled Santa Claus if he went on a bender after spending too much time hanging out in the chimneys. Lester managed the Wilson Marina, if one used the verb in the loosest sense of the word. Jackie owned the ship store there. She was equally round in the belly, but a little more well-kempt. Her graying hair hung in loose curls around her face and fell to her shoulders. It was her eyes that sent an involuntary shiver down my spine when our gazes happened to cross. The slate gray resembled cold steel. Maybe she was the brains behind Lester's flabby brawn? Speculation ran rampant in Wilson over how Lester managed to keep his job despite numerous fines being levied against him, both by the Homeowner's Association (HOA) and the Fish and Wildlife Commission.

She took her place and cleared her throat. "Thank you, Robert, and thank you, citizens of Wilson. I have been a law-abiding, God-fearing member of the Wilson community for almost a decade now. I, along with my brother, understand the delicate balance between the economy and ecology of our fine neighborhood. I will work tirelessly to preserve the beauty of Lake Amore and the town of Wilson."

Her declaration was met with gagging sounds from Denise, who stood and chimed in. "You and your brother are only concerned about your bottom line as evidenced by the disrepair of the marina and the jacked-up prices in your store. What I am sure of is that any policies you push will only serve your profit margins and interests."

Denise's squad cheered, earning them a glare from both Jackie and Robert. Thankfully, though, no one said anything further and Jackie took her seat. Robert looked like he needed a drink in the worst possible way. "I will ask for order as we honor our last candidate. Ms. Tucker, would you please make your statement."

Tessa stood, her shoulder-length brown hair swaying slightly with the movement. It was one of the few times I'd ever seen it down. Her work in the bakery and pastry shop meant it was secured above her head and covered with a hair net most days. She took a moment to survey the crowd and offered a genuine smile toward each section. The corner of her mouth quirked into a grin. "Well, Mr. President, I'm not sure what else is left to say after all of that."

Muffled chuckles spread throughout the crowd. One had to love her sense of humor and candor. I caught her gaze and nodded in encouragement to continue. She exhaled and pulled out a notecard from her pocket. "I hope you don't mind if I refer to my notes. I get a little nervous in front of large crowds, but this is important to me, so I wanted to make sure I got it right." Another deep breath. "I am a local business owner, supporter of the community for over a decade, and looking to protect the interest of all Wilsonites. My goal is to represent you and the interests that are most important to you. I have no personal agenda other than to ensure the continued peace and prosperity of our little slice of heaven nestled here in the heart of Lake Amore."

I clapped, and many others followed. I think her non-grandiose way of speaking to and about everyone here made them enjoy the lack of drama in her statement. She nodded her thanks and took her seat. Denise's expression was one of respect and concern. She probably suspected Tessa provided the most serious competition for her. But with three seats available, I thought they both stood a decent chance. Tessa had one of my votes for sure, though.

Robert brought the attention to himself one final time. "Thank you to all the candidates who shared with us tonight and to you for coming out to hear their statements. Please do your research and consider carefully who will get your vote. You may cast your votes online or drop your sealed ballot off at the CIA building. Results will be posted Friday with polls closing at midnight Thursday. Thank you and good evening."

Once I'd managed to make it outside, Kelsey gave me a quick hug. Before she could head home, I took her hand to keep her with me. "So, what do you think about Karen withdrawing? Not that I'm disappointed, but something is up. I can't stop thinking about who sent the message. It couldn't have been Jackie as she didn't appear to have a phone or any other communication device with her."

"I'm not sure, Sadie. Though, I suspect there is

probably technology that will allow you to schedule messages to be sent at a specific time."

I nodded. "Yes, I'm sure there is. However, the timing of the message was too spot on to have been something she guessed ahead of time. There was no way to know how long each candidate would talk, or even in what order. No, I think someone else sent the message. The question is who."

"And why," Kelsey added.

"The why is definitely important here," I agreed.

"I'll see what I can find out. In the meantime, enjoy your evening, I'll talk to you tomorrow."

I made the short trip to my truck, lost in my own thoughts. This was certainly an evening people would talk about for some time to come. Emerson was standing at the door of my truck when I walked up. I pulled him into a fierce hug. "You've got some explaining to do, mister. I've been worried about you!"

"I know. I'm sorry, Ms. Sadie. I just needed time to process."

After releasing him, I nodded. "That's understandable. Want to tell me what happened? What in the world were you doing in the woods next to Lakeside Condos so early in the morning?"

His dark brown eyes found something in the parking lot incredibly fascinating at that exact moment. I'd never known him to be shy, at least not around me. We'd hit it off almost from the beginning and had been partners in crime—or more like solving crimes—ever since. I squeezed his shoulder in support. Finally, he spoke. "It's sort of my auntie's fault."

My face scrunched into disbelief. With an index finger, I lifted his chin so our gazes met again. "Your Aunt Isabella made you go out by yourself in the wee hours of the morning?"

He sighed. "Not exactly."

Ah, the joys of teenage evasion. I did the same thing (and some might say I still do) when I was a kid. Not sure why my parents didn't strangle me. "Then, maybe you should elaborate."

"Auntie's ideas about earning money are a little different than most people."

His statement did nothing to ease my confusion or understanding of why he was at a murder scene. "Your aunt owns a flower shop. I'm pretty sure she has at least some interest in monetary ways."

My statement caused a small grin to emerge. "That's fair, but not when it comes to teaching me life lessons."

Now, my interest was piqued. "Tell me more."

"I want an electric scooter. It will make it easier to get around and I can even save time delivering flowers for her in the neighborhood."

I nodded. "That seems reasonable. I'm still not sure how this is all connected, though. Her wanting you to earn money for the scooter makes sense."

He sighed. "She will provide the money if I think of and act on ways to improve myself, my family, and my community. So, I figured picking up trash in the neighborhood would qualify as helping my community."

His aunt was doing a great job teaching him the important things in life. "I think that's a wonderful idea. You were picking up trash in the woods when you ran across Miles, right?"

Emerson nodded. "I've never seen a dead body before." His head dropped. "Well, unless you count my parents' funeral."

I embraced him tightly. "I'm so sorry, Emerson. Sorry for your parents and sorry you had to experience the nightmare of discovering a body." Pulling back a bit, I asked, "Are you doing all right? Is there anything I can do to help?"

He exhaled slowly. "For now, you can provide some distraction. Until the forum tonight, it's been the only thing I can think about."

I smiled. "I can do that. So, what did you think of tonight's soap opera?"

"Soap opera?"

I laughed. "Never mind. You've probably never seen, much less heard, of one. Someday over lunch, I'll bring you up to speed on the latest of All My Children or General Hospital. Though, to be honest, it's been so long since I've watched daytime television, they might not even be on anymore."

He chuckled and shook his head. "Whatever you say. As for what I thought about tonight, I need to review my notes and think on it a bit more before sharing."

His response both impressed and amused me. I really wished there were some other kids his age who lived in Wilson. I assumed he had friends at school, but given how mature his thinking typically was, maybe he didn't fit in there. The death of his parents had made him grow up too fast. "That's fair. Maybe as you're reviewing your notes and thoughts, you can figure out why Karen Bizzy withdrew her candidacy. That would be another way you could help your community."

He laughed. "I'm pretty sure her withdrawal all by itself helps the community."

The kid was smart. "You're not wrong." I wished there was something I could do to help him. Then, a thought occurred to me. "One way you can help yourself is talking to someone about your parents, about Miles, and about life in general."

I didn't regret my words, but I did hate that the smile left his face. "Auntie had me talk to some guy for about a year after they died. He said until I accepted their deaths and moved on, I couldn't fully heal."

The therapist wasn't wrong, but telling someone who couldn't have been more than twelve to move on from the loss of his parents was a pretty tall order. Heck, I'm not sure I could do that at thirty. "And you aren't even ready to begin thinking about accepting it, are you?"

"Not until I find out what really happened to them."

The conviction in his voice reaffirmed my desire to

help him find out the truth. "We will someday, my friend. We will."

He let out a slow breath before straightening to his full height. He must have had a growth spurt while I wasn't looking as he was only four or five inches shorter than me now. I studied him more closely. "You need to stop growing. What are you now, five foot five?"

He laughed. "Five foot six, to be exact."

"You have been growing while I wasn't looking. Stop that!" I teased.

My words made him laugh, which was my goal. "Yes, ma'am. I'll see what I can do about that."

"Good man! Have a great night, Emerson. I'm always available if you want to talk, day or night. Okay?"

"Yes, ma'am. You have a good night, too, Ms. Sadie."

I watched him walk away, reminding myself he was only a kid. A very mature and smart kid, but still someone who needed extra TLC in the coming days and weeks. Before he got too far, I raised my voice to get his attention. "Hey, Emerson!"

He stopped and turned around. "Yes?"

"Let's have lunch sometime this week. We'll review your notes and catch up." It would give me the perfect opportunity to make sure he was doing okay.

"I have school."

Oh, right, that would interfere with lunch plans. "After school snack, then?"

He laughed. "Sounds good. I'll text you."

Having settled that, I hopped in my truck with thoughts swirling in my mind about everything that had happened in the past forty-eight hours. It was a lot. I would need to be like Emerson and organize and review my notes to keep it all straight in my head.

When I pulled up to the house, I noticed someone sitting on the steps leading up to the front door. It was Natalie. I parked in the driveway without opening the garage and walked up to her. "What's wrong?" It didn't take someone adept at reading people to see she was furious.

"Dante has been arrested."

Chapter Six

"Arrested for Miles' murder?" It was probably obvious but I thought it best to confirm.

"Yes, and it's all your fault!" Her slim finger punched my chest. She didn't need to clarify. No one else was around (thankfully).

I stepped back a couple paces to create some distance. She'd demonstrated earlier today that Dante had taught her a thing or two. I'd rather not find myself laying on the ground again at her mercy. "How is it my fault?"

She crossed her arms and shot me a look of bewilderment. "How can you even ask such a stupid question?!"

"I figure it's always better to go straight to the source than try to guess."

"You are unbelievable. You self-righteous...ugh! If you'd made sure Miles spent the rest of his life in jail for his crimes, none of this would have happened. Not only did you fail us on that job, but then a job or two later, you left us! You abandoned our family. You don't care about us at all!"

Rather than a young woman in her mid-twenties, she sounded like a rebellious teenager who'd just been grounded. It was hard to rationalize with someone so angry, but I had to try. I softened my voice and took a tentative step toward her. "It's because I cared so much, I suggested we go our separate ways for a while. I was trying to protect you."

"Well, we can see how well that's worked, haven't we?" Natalie scoffed. "Dante is suspected of murder. You and I both know he would never kill anyone."

"I'm still trying to process him beating the crap out of Miles. He rarely did things like that. Which means his pattern has either changed or something else is going on. Violence begets violence."

"How dare you lecture me! It's time to choose, Sadie. Either your new life or the family you put together all those years ago. What's it gonna be?"

Anger oozed from every pore of Natalie's being. I'd never seen her this upset. While I still intended to try to build myself a new life, I couldn't leave Dante in jail for a crime I was *almost* positive he didn't commit. I still wasn't sure about Natalie, but the truth needed to be discovered before any of us could move forward. My gaze met Nat's and sought to convey warmth and trust. "Let's figure this out. You and me. We'll find whoever really killed Miles and get Dante released."

I expected relief, gratitude–something. Instead, she simply nodded. "Where do you want to start?"

I wanted to start with a glass of wine and a good night's sleep, but that wasn't what Natalie wanted to hear. Maybe I could have both of those things, but it wasn't going to be anytime soon. "Why don't you come in? We'll have a glass of wine or whatever you want to drink and discuss a game plan."

After entirely too long of a pause, she finally nodded. "Okay."

I disarmed the security system, and we went inside. Once our drinks and a snack had been procured, we sat down in the living room. "Nice place you got here."

"It's how I spent part of the nest egg we had." I left out that she could have had a nice place, too, if she hadn't been acting like a vigilante following some guy across the country to make a point. That statement would, most likely, end our temporary truce.

She nodded. "So, what's the plan? That's your department, I recall."

A small sigh escaped. I had been the one to mastermind our jobs, but over the past six months I'd enjoyed not being responsible for the lives of so many with each decision I made. It was a difficult burden to bear. While I liked being the one making the decisions (I might have some control issues...), the break had been good for my mental health. "I'm going to go visit Dante tomorrow morning and I need you to pull together whatever evidence you've collected to prove Miles was up to no good again."

"What makes you think I have evidence?"

"I would hope after following him around for the past six months or so and, apparently, making his life a living hell, you would at least have some proof!"

Nat set her drink down and crossed her arms in a huff. "I'm working on it."

The urge to rub my temples in frustration won out. I needed a moment to collect myself. After a long breath, my gaze met hers. "Then, work harder. Even though Miles is gone, he may have been working with someone to carry out his alleged evil plans."

"Not alleged!"

"Without proof, it remains solidly in the alleged classification."

"Fine. I'll work on getting the proof. You talk to Dante and find the real killer."

The silence stretched on for fifteen minutes. I made use of the time to work out what I was going to say to Dante and how best to deal with Nat. There was still something giving me an uneasy feeling, but I couldn't put my finger on it. Whatever 'it' was, it wasn't good, though. I still trusted my gut enough to know at least that much was true.

Once finished with my wine, I looked over to Nat. She had left her glass on the table, leaned back on the couch, and her eyes were closed. Like this, she looked so young and innocent. At twenty-six, she'd seen a lot of things already in her short life. Some good, but too much bad. I'd met her on the set of a foreign film about five years ago. She had given up her dream of being a gymnast so she could work to help her family pay bills. Because she had been very athletic, bendy (as her parents had often told her), and, most importantly, fearless, she'd gotten hired as a stunt double. I'd seen something in her, something more than where her life was taking her. She could use the skills she had for more than entertainment. I offered her a job and she left the film company to become part of our rag-tag team.

Everything had gone well until she begged us to go to California to battle Cal-Ag and Miles Grant. We stopped his unauthorized testing of a new and dangerous pesticide that was causing the farmers in the test fields to get violently ill as a result. Some of those affected included Nat's grandparents. We also learned he'd been skimming money from his company to fund his unauthorized research.

In theory, the job was successful. We proved Miles' involvement, got him fired, took his money, and he spent a small amount of time in a prison for the rich—one of those country club lockdown places. In reality, Nat had wanted him to do hard time for the rest of his life. I'd thought she'd accepted the outcome and moved on. It was safe to say I was wrong.

Leaning over, I gently touched her on the knee. "Hey, you got a place to stay? You're welcome to stay here."

Her light blue gaze held mine for a moment before she shook her head. "Appreciate the offer, but I'm good."

It was no surprise she wouldn't accept an act of

kindness. My role was to find the real killer and then let them move on with their lives. I guess that's what I wanted, too. Everything felt so jumbled right now. "Okay. How will I reach you?"

She stood, stretched, and grabbed the cross-body bag she always had with her. "You won't. I'll reach you."

It was my turn to act a little petulant. "Fine. Talk soon."

"Yup."

Without so much as a goodbye, she headed out the door. Oh, how things had changed.

Monday morning arrived entirely too early. Another night that rest had been a shifty stranger. I couldn't say I didn't sleep at all, but the amount of concealer required to hide the dark circles under my eyes indicated it wasn't enough or of adequate quality to count for much.

Adrenaline surged through my veins when I realized my truck wasn't in the garage. Where could it be? I pressed the button to open the garage door as I made the call to 911. Maybe Nat had figured a way around my security system and stole my truck to teach me a lesson. I wouldn't put it past her.

Once the garage door finished lifting, the voice came on the phone. "911, what is your emergency?"

I started to open my mouth, but the sight of my

truck sitting in the driveway reminded me I'd been distracted by Natalie being on my front steps last night. "I'm so sorry, false alarm."

"Ma'am, are you sure we can't be of assistance? Are you not free to talk?"

Guilt filled my veins as the adrenaline disappeared. "I'm truly sorry. I thought my truck had been stolen, but I found it. Thank you for your concern and quick answer to the call."

"It is my job, ma'am."

She probably thought I'd been drinking all night and forgot where I parked. The last part was true, but only one glass of wine had shared the evening with me. "Yes, thank you, ma'am. Have a nice day."

The emergency operator hung up, most likely annoyed I'd kept her from someone who really needed help. Oh yes, this day was starting off in a stellar way. Now that my heart rate had returned to normal, I noticed a bright yellow flyer stuck in the windshield wiper of my truck. I pulled it out and almost dropped my coffee as I read the highlights:

Be careful who you cast your vote for. Know the facts! Alan Knightly voted against municipal utilities for the RV park. His vote meant increased danger to the eco-balance of Lake Amore and potential pollution for our community. Is that who we want leading us?

The text was accompanied by a black and white picture of Alan along with one of Lake Amore and a hazardous waste symbol imposed over the image. Oh, the joys of local politics. Despite the dramatics of it all, the accusation surprised me. While Alan had lodged serious concerns over the RV park, EZ had told me most of it was just to argue with Ted Birmingham and keep him on his toes. I also wondered how anyone outside the board would know how the members voted. Maybe they used the old, "All in favor, say aye. Those opposed, say nay. The nays have it." Regardless, someone was doing their best to make sure Alan didn't get the votes needed for re-election.

Alan's plight was not my concern. I was on my way to visit Dante, and that took precedence over everything else. I needed to look him in the eye when I asked my questions. Was he arrested simply because he'd had an altercation with Miles preceding his death? Or was there another reason? I needed to hear the truth, though I'm not sure I wanted it.

The drive to the Crockett County Government Complex took about thirty minutes or so in morning rush hour traffic. Thankfully, Dante wasn't being held in Houston as that would have probably tripled my commute time. Most of the drivers were polite (at least compared to other big cities I'd been around), but the sheer number of them always meant it took at least twice as long to get somewhere.

The complex had a large parking lot surrounded by a few buildings that housed various governmental entities, including both the game warden's office and the county jail, which were separated by two other buildings. I wasn't certain what agencies were located there. A beautiful sculpture in a courtyard filled with greenery and flowers made one question if it really was winter at all.

After a few calming breaths, I left the safety of my vehicle and made my way to the county jail. The lady at the receptionist desk looked out of place as a gate-keeper for a jail. Her salt and pepper hair framed her round, cherub-like face. Kind gray eyes greeted me with a smile. "Good morning, ma'am, how may I help you?"

I noted from the carved wooden block on the desk her name was Agnes Merigold. "Good morning, Ms. Merigold. I'd like to see Dante Miller, if I may." Might as well put my Southern manners on full display this morning.

"Are you his attorney?"

The desire to spin a tale was strong. However, I hadn't planned ahead enough to bring false credentials from my treasure trove of secret identities. Truthfully, I didn't want to lie to her. On her desk was a picture of what appeared to be a much younger Agnes with a group of friends. They were at a baseball game, maybe even an Astros home game. Keeping this picture on her desk alongside those of her family (the resemblance was easy to see in those photos) indicated to me she held friendship in very high esteem. That detail gave me my angle. I gestured to the chair in front of her desk. "May I sit?"

She nodded. "Of course."

I leaned forward, allowing some of the desperation I felt on the inside to show on my face. "He's an old friend who has found himself in a lot of trouble. I posted bail for him just a couple days ago. I understand he's been accused of some pretty bad stuff. Maybe it's a younger me that hopes to reach him, to understand what he might have been thinking over the past few days to see if I can, in some way, help him. I promise to only take a few moments and am happy to follow any security protocols you deem appropriate."

Her expression softened as her brows knitted in concentration. I held very still, not wanting to disrupt her thought process. I could only hope my side was winning the internal battle. Finally, she reached into her drawer and pulled out a clipboard and laid it on the desk in front of her. "Since Mr. Miller hasn't been formerly charged and it's been a very busy morning catching up from the weekend, I haven't had the opportunity to complete his intake paperwork. If I were to allow you to visit him, say for a quarter of an hour, this form would need to be completed first. Understood?"

Her message was received loud and clear. "I understand. I'm happy to help so you can tend to other responsibilities."

Her smile and nod indicated I'd picked up what she was laying down. "Well, that would be wonderful. Thank you." She handed me the clipboard and a pen. "If you'll come with me."

As I followed her past the locked door to a room with no windows, the phrase Emerson was always reminding me of, *The truth will set you free,* might have had more merit than I initially gave it credit. I remembered Emerson laughing and telling me the quote was from the Bible, not him personally. Regardless of the origin, the phrase was settling further into my thought processes. Though I knew telling the truth didn't always get the results one desired, today it had given me access I previously would have conned my way into. Maybe the kid was on to something.

A moment later, Dante was led into the room. There were no cuffs, and he still had his street clothes on. Agnes was telling the truth as well. He hadn't been charged...yet. That detail gave me hope. The jeans and graphic T-shirt looked much better on him than the standard orange most prisoners wore. Orange was definitely not his color.

As soon as the guard left the room, I glanced over the paper. "I need you to quickly answer these questions so I can fulfill my promise to the sweet receptionist who let me back here to speak with you." My gaze pierced his, and a small part of my heart crinkled at the forlorn expression he wore. He'd looked that way the last time I saw him, too. I reached over and put my hand over his. "Then, we can talk in the time I have left. Okay?"

He nodded.

The routine paperwork was dispensed with quickly and I moved on to my true purpose for being there. "Agnes says you haven't been charged with murder yet. Correct?"

Dante nodded his head but offered nothing more.

He took the strong, silent type a bit too far in my opin-ion. "Then, why are you here?"

"For questioning. Suspicion of murder."

I would need to provide Natalie a little lecture on the differences between being arrested and brought in for questioning. "Because of your previous altercation with Miles." I'd made sure the question inflection was nowhere in my voice when I made that statement. These facts weren't up for debate.

He nodded again, anyway.

"Did you kill him?" The question had to be asked, even though it pained me to do so.

The same hurt I'd seen in Natalie's gaze at the question showed in his expression. Though, his was minus the same anger and rage I'd witnessed in hers. He waited several beats before he answered. "What do you think?"

I shrugged. "I don't believe you did."

We let the tension remain in the air for a few moments before I asked my next question. "Why did you leave my house in the middle of the night? I could have given you an alibi."

"Did you ask Nat if she killed that snake?"

"I did."

"You used to trust us, had our backs."

I covered both of his large hands with mine. "I still do, but you have to admit the circumstances and timing look bad for both of you."

He said nothing, so I continued. "Where did you

go after you left my house? Maybe I can provide an alibi another way."

"You'll figure it out. You taught us well."

His inability to give me a straight answer was wearing on my already tired nerves. "That tells me nothing, and Dante..." I squeezed his hands a little tighter, "I'm trying to have your back. Help me, help you."

He offered nothing more, so we spent the remaining few minutes we had together in silence. When Agnes knocked on the door, I stood. "If I'd taught you anything at all, you wouldn't be sitting here right now."

My words had their desired effect as a flash of pain and hurt crossed his sullen features. "Take care, Dante."

Right before I opened the door to exit, I heard, "Sadie."

I turned. "Yes?"

"Remember the Zig Zag job?"

I remembered the name of the job, but the details eluded me. As there was no time to discuss it further, I simply answered. "Yes."

"Me too."

Okay, that was odd, but I didn't want to take advantage of Agnes' understanding nature and kindness. "Goodbye, my old friend."

"Sadie."

I closed my eyes momentarily, fighting back all the emotion trying to escape. This time, I didn't turn around. "Yes?"

"Be smart."

At his statement, tears threatened. I needed to get out of there. "Always," I managed before escaping the pain of the room and my old life. No, that wasn't true. My old life had been wonderful. Together, my team and I accomplished a great many things in the name of real justice. True, our methods often colored outside the lines–okay, sometimes they weren't even on the same page as the lines–but we got results by using our wits and understanding of human nature to achieve results. Before we'd leave to go out on any job, our standard departure statement was, "Be smart." It reminded us to keep our wits about us and think on our feet. That was the best way to avoid trouble.

I handed Agnes the clipboard. "Thank you, Ms. Merigold, for the time and for your understanding. Here's the information you needed."

Wise old eyes studied me for a moment before she reached over and clasped my forearm. "For what it's worth, despite his appearance, I don't sense murderous intent from him. And, believe me, I've been around enough criminals in my lifetime to know the guilty from the innocent. Your friend isn't one hundred percent innocent, but he's not a killer, either."

The moisture in my eyes spilled over the edge. Just a few drops, but enough to know I needed to get out of there. "I hope so, ma'am. I truly do."

With that, I quickly made my leave, not wanting anyone else to witness my emotional break. I'd almost made it to my truck when Jeremy caught up with me. "Sadie, what are you doing here?"

His unending questions about my motives, my location, and my life grinded on what little patience I had left. "Is this not an area for the public?" My words came out harsher than I intended, but right now I didn't care.

He recoiled slightly from my tone. "Yes, but I'm worried about you. An early morning visit to the county jail is never a good thing, unless you're an attorney." Horror slid across his face. "You didn't pretend to be an attorney, did you?"

Anger simmered just below the surface. "Since you obviously have a spy in the building, why don't you ask him or her?"

He exhaled slowly. Through my watery gaze, it looked like he was trying to regain his composure. "I'm just worried about you. Is trouble knocking at your door again?"

How could I not have seen how incompatible we were? While I knew he was worried about me, it felt like he always assumed the worst about me or my situation. And who was I kidding? His standards were impeccable, and I couldn't see myself living up to them. Right then, at that moment, I was tired of trying. "More like knocking down the door. Listen, I have to go. See you around, Jeremy."

I heard him calling my name as I started the truck. Quickly, I turned the music up so I couldn't make out what he was saying. It was a total teenage move, which

I would undoubtedly regret later. Right now, though, I needed to leave.

One last look in my rearview mirror saw him standing there, hands on those narrow, muscular hips as his head shook in dismay. It was for the best. I didn't have time in my life for such frivolity. A romantic relationship, or even one that I pretended wasn't potential romance at all, was not in the cards. It was time I moved on from that fantasy.

Some place quiet to think–that's what I needed. Had Dante been trying to tell me something without really telling me? He'd never been one to talk in riddles, but today he did. I had to believe it was his way of warning me. His way of urging me to figure this out.

My lungs drew in oxygen and let it out slowly. Yes, this was the new plan: Figure this out, make sure Dante was not actually arrested, restore my relationship with Natalie, and then try, once again, to move forward.

I sighed as a few more errant tears fell down my face. It was going to be a long day.

Chapter Seven

Once back in Wilson, I pulled myself together and opened Tesoro. It was a later start than usual, but since I was my own boss, I approved the time off. Sole proprietorship had to have some benefits, right?

I'd been open less than an hour when I decided it was time to make some notes. I retrieved my notebook and read over what I had before adding anything new:

Miles changed his last name and convinced James Cutter to invest in a new business.

James made an initial investment. Possibly other investors as well. Potential that one of the investors (most likely James?) was going to invest about a month after the deal was drawn up. No idea why.

Time of death estimated between 4 and 5 a.m. Saturday morning.

Miles likely knew his attacker.

Dante left my home sometime in the middle of the night.

Odd piece of yellow plastic found in the wooded area where the murder occurred.

Natalie had made it her mission to make Miles' life difficult.

My breath shuddered as I released it after reading over the notes. I almost hated to write the next things down, but it had to be done:

Plastic ring most likely belonged to Nat—she was there!

Dante taken in for questioning—suspicion of murder.

Dante tells me to be smart and to remember Zig Zag job.

I sighed. I hadn't really learned much of anything in the last thirty-six or so hours. I had to do better. The problem was, I had no idea where to start. I'd told Dante I remembered the job, but the details were sketchy. For logical reasons, we hadn't kept comprehensive logs. Less evidence, should we ever be caught. I would need to remember the details and understand why they were important. There had to be a reason. As a man of few words, the ones he did say typically held significant meaning.

Before I could devote my brain power to figuring out anything more, the bell rang, signaling a customer. "Hi, Denise. See something yesterday and returning to make a purchase?" I grinned.

She didn't smile. Instead, she marched over to stand in front of me. Her blonde hair swayed with each determined step. Blue eyes filled with fury prompted me to send up a quick prayer that I wasn't the source of her aggravation. I'm not sure my emotional bandwidth could take much more. "Can you believe the audacity of some people?"

I could not. Especially, since I had no idea who she was talking about. I didn't want to engage in the latest round of town gossip, but I'd not seen her this upset before, so I put aside the priorities clawing at my brain and gave her my attention. "Tell me what happened."

She waved the yellow flyer in the air. "This! This is what happened."

Ah yes. I figured I wasn't the only one to receive this tidbit of information about Alan. To say I was relieved this was the source of her fury was an understatement. "Is it true?"

She slammed the flyer down on the counter and crossed her arms in a huff. "I don't know. But I'll tell you this: I'm going straight to the source. If he says it's false, then my sole mission in life is to find out who started this little smear campaign and put an end to it."

It sounded like a good plan to me. "What's your next step?" Since I had no idea what I was going to do next other than try to remember things I'd relegated to a box at the back of the long-term storage in my brain, I might as well listen to someone else's plans. Who knows, maybe an idea would come from it all.

"I'm going to meet Alan for a drink and ask him."

She made the statement like there was no other option. "And if he lies?"

Denise's head shook. "I've studied that man long and hard enough. I'll know if he's lying."

I gifted her with a frown. "Some call that stalking."

The anger in her blue gaze now twinkled as a smile crept across her face for the first time since walking in the store. "Not if he likes it." She winked.

The courts might disagree should Alan ever change stances on his stalker, but as they say here in Texas (or maybe I just said it): Not my cowboy, not my rodeo. If Denise wasn't worried about the potential outcome, neither would I. "Fair enough. Keep me posted. I'm curious about several events surrounding this election."

"Politics is an ugly business. I'm not sure I want to be a part of it, after all."

"Agreed. Between Karen's weird behavior, JB's even odder behavior, and now this, maybe I underestimated the power of the board here in Wilson. People seem willing to do anything to get one of those seats."

Denise sighed heavily, all the usual fire and flirt absent. "Right now, I just want to get at the truth and show support for someone I consider a friend."

Moving from behind the counter, I offered her a quick hug. "I have no doubts you'll do just that."

After a deep breath, she smiled. "Darn tootin' I will. Ain't nobody messin' with my man."

"Atta girl," I laughed, happy to see her back to normal. "Now, go and find out the truth!"

"Thanks, Sadie." She made her way toward the door. She was almost out when she turned. "You do the same."

Before I could say anything, she was gone. She was right. I needed to learn the truth about what happened to Miles, even if it might cost me friends from my past and jeopardize my future.

Moving back to the counter and my comfy seat, I took out a piece of paper and started making notes of what I remembered from all the jobs my team and I had done over the past decade or so (which I would shred later). This was going to require a lot of caffeine!

A few hours later and, to be honest, not much in the way of information gleaned from my tired brain, I closed up shop. In my defense, there had been a decent crowd this afternoon. Apparently EZ's modeling of her recently purchased earrings was having a nice effect. Not only were her co-workers shopping but, interestingly enough, a few men came in to buy something for their wives. Now, I couldn't be one hundred percent certain they'd been prompted by seeing them on EZ, but whether it was pure coincidence or they were making amends for their after-hours activities, a sale was a sale. I had enough problems of my own right now to ensure I didn't try to fix any marriages or set men who had gone astray on the straight and narrow.

I may not have had much success finding information from the past, but an idea had occurred to me about how to get some from the present. After locking up and turning on the security system–hey, Nat was out there somewhere and she was a gifted thief–I texted Kelsey. *Can I come by tonight to see you and Pete? I'll bring tequila.*

A few moments later, my phone beeped with a reply. *He will love that. Come for dinner. 6:30.*

That was a nice bonus I would gladly accept. The thought of trying to make a meal for one tonight held no appeal. *Sounds good. See you then.*

On my way home to change before heading to the liquor store to pick up Pete's favorite tequila, I couldn't help but drive by Lakeside Condos. My heart stopped, as did my truck, when I saw a swarm of police cars and uniformed officers combing through the woods in a standard grid search pattern. Don't ask me how I knew what that was.

It felt like several days had passed since Miles' murder but, in reality, it had only been about forty-eight hours. That was a long time to let a crime scene sit before doing a thorough search of the area. His murder might not be a top priority, but still. A couple days was more than enough time for someone to inadvertently (or one hundred percent on purpose) contaminate the crime scene.

Guilt surged through my body. I *had* tampered with it by removing the yellow plastic ring. I hadn't known at the time it was Natalie's. Regardless, the police frowned on anything or anyone disturbing a taped off crime scene area, whether it was relevant or not. In this case, I feared it could potentially point them to the killer. Nat had said she didn't do it, but she could also be lying. It wouldn't be a stretch, someone not telling the truth to avoid being a prime suspect in a murder.

There was another possibility, however. Maybe there had been new evidence discovered that prompted them to search again? It wasn't unheard of. Maybe they knew what they were looking for now? Maybe there was something tying the killer to the scene? The knot in my stomach twisted and squeezed. I needed to figure out a way to share the evidence I'd taken without getting myself brought in for questioning like Dante.

After adding that to the very long list of things to worry about, I continued with my current objective: Obtain tequila, give tequila to Pete, and, most importantly, get Pete to tell me what he knew about the business deal his firm was going to broker for Miles.

Pete and Kelsey's home was situated at the top of a rather steep driveway. Another benefit to living in Texas, there wasn't much snow and ice to contend with. In Nebraska, where I grew up, this layout would be a death trap for those charged with clearing the driveway. Heck, with the ice, you wouldn't even be able to get up the driveway to the garage. Thankfully, that wasn't an issue here in the South.

It was a one-story brick home with nice landscaping. While not lakefront, they could still claim lakeview. The true allure, however, was the fact it sat on two lots. On a peninsula, real estate was a precious commodity. Wilson already utilized zero lot lines to maximize the number of homes they could build on the land. The wooded areas (like the one Miles was found in) had steadily been dwindling at a pace that made me more than a little nervous. All of this meant rising costs for each square foot. It was the age-old supply and demand principle. The fact that Pete and Kelsey's home sat on two of these prime spots meant they were, minimally, at a comfortable level financially.

Pete answered the door when I rang. "Hey, Sadie. Come on in."

"Thanks, Pete." I lifted the brown paper bag. "I come bearing gifts."

He took the bag from me and peeked inside. His eyes lit up simultaneously as his lips curled into a satisfied smile. "Nice gift. For me?"

"Yes. I've heard it's been a bit of a difficult and possibly disappointing past few days for you. Thought this might make things better, at least for a while."

He pulled the white bottle with blue flowers on it out of the bag. Lifting it to the light with appreciation, he replied, "This makes even a good day better. Thanks."

"You're welcome."

About that time, Kelsey emerged from the kitchen. "Hi, Sadie. Dinner's about ready. Want a glass of wine?"

"I thought we'd do a shot first. That is, if Pete's okay with sharing."

He pretended to think it over. "Well, since I always have to share with my wife..."

Kelsey flashed him a warning shot. "Which you love doing. Right, dear?"

Pete laughed. "Of course, babe. What's mine is yours."

"And what's mine is mine," she finished.

I laughed at their banter. This was obviously not the first time they'd had this exchange. We moved the party into the kitchen/dining room area. While Pete arranged the drinks, Kelsey turned her attention to me. "How are you doing?"

The temptation to whitewash everything was great, but Kelsey had shown me unwavering support since day one. She deserved the truth—or at least as much as I could give her. "It's been a long day, a long several days, and it's only Monday of a new week."

"It has been rather eventful, hasn't it?"

Not wanting to go into any further details of my day, at least until after dinner, I reached into my purse and pulled out the yellow flyer. "You get one of these today?"

She took the piece of paper. "No, but I saw it online in the community Facebook group. Someone has been very busy since the forum."

"Thoughts on who?"

Before she could answer, Pete arrived with the shot glasses dressed and filled with the clear liquid along with lemons and limes on the side. We each took a glass and raised them in anticipation of a toast. Pete took the lead. "Here's to hoping life doesn't continue to suck the rest of the week."

"Pete!" Kelsey admonished. "Seriously, that's the best you can do?"

He cut her a look. "We're doing shots of tequila on a Monday. If that doesn't say life has sucked recently, I don't know what does."

Kelsey rolled her eyes, but she chuckled. "I suppose you have a point."

"To life not sucking." I raised my glass again.

"To life not sucking!" Pete and Kelsey repeated.

We licked the salt, downed the shot, and took our fruit of choice. Though, to be honest, the tequila was so smooth, it didn't really require the citrus follow-up. But, hey, when in Rome...

"Another?" Pete smiled.

"Maybe after dinner. Let's go eat," Kelsey advised before he could get too excited about the prospect of some more liquid comfort.

"Fine," he huffed. "But only because you made my favorite."

The grilled salmon was accompanied by roasted fingerling potatoes and asparagus. My stomach growled in response to the smells. "Kelsey, this looks amazing!"

"My woman can cook." Pete pulled her close and pressed a hard kiss to her cheek. He then offered the lascivious grin I was accustomed to seeing on his face. "Amongst other things," he added.

"Pete!"

He laughed. "Take the compliment, babe. Let's eat."

We enjoyed several bites in relative silence before Kelsey resumed our conversation. "To answer your earlier question, Sadie, logic says it must be an enemy of Alan's. It was mean spirited and violated multiple rules of conduct when it comes to what is public knowledge regarding individual votes by board members."

"So, if the target was Alan Knightly, that leads me right to the doorstep of the Birmingham family. It's not a big secret they don't like each other."

"True, but they would have to know they'd be the prime suspect. Given how much the Birminghams protect their reputation, does it make sense to be so obvious?"

I sighed. "No, but sometimes the obvious is, well, obvious for a reason."

"Maybe it was the same person who did the number on Bizzy-body," Pete shared before taking another bite.

Kelsey nodded. "It's a possibility, but a common enemy of both Karen and Alan? They don't really run in the same social circles. The Birminghams are at the top of the social ladder in any circle around here. Karen is more off to the side on a step stool trying to get people to notice her. They have money, but that's about as far as their influence takes them."

"Someone should tell her that," Pete scoffed.

I wanted to fuss at him, but he had a point. "Denise stopped by the shop earlier today. She was as mad as

I've ever seen her. I think we can trust that she's going to get to the bottom of this issue."

"Well, she does have the hots for Knightly," Pete commented.

Kelsey laughed. "That's the worst kept secret in Wilson."

"You're not wrong." I finished the last of the food on my plate. "Kelsey, that was fantastic. Thank you for the dinner invite."

"It was my pleasure. I worry you don't eat enough."

This week, she might have been right, but normally, between my favorite pasta, yogurt, and Tessa's Texas gold bars, I provided myself with more than enough calories to get through the day. "Some weeks are better than others."

She nodded. "No argument there." After the dishes were finished, I decided the timing might be right to start my quest for the needed information. "I know things have been tough for you, Pete. I'm sorry about your deal."

He sighed, grabbed a bottle of wine instead of the tequila, and headed to the living room. "Grab a glass, we'll talk. Since it is only Monday, we'll save another round of the good stuff for the weekend."

This was either Pete being very responsible or, more likely, not wanting to share any more of his gift. It was hard to fault him for that logic. Once seated and the wine poured, I kicked off the conversation. "What happens to the deal now? After Miles' death?"

Pete took a sip of wine. I could tell he was thinking hard. He sighed and closed his eyes, either to compose himself or because he was merely deep in thought. I shot a glance at Kelsey, who lifted her index finger. I waited.

A minute or so later, he sat up and opened his eyes. "You have no common legal interest with the client, right?"

My interest was only personal and not related to the law except to find his killer. I nodded. "Right."

"Then, I can use the common interest exception to privilege to give you at least a few details."

I had no idea what that really meant, but I trusted Pete knew what he was talking about. "I appreciate that. Whatever you share stays between the three of us." I might use what he told me to form opinions on other matters, but the details of this deal would not be shared with anyone else.

Satisfied with my response, Pete leaned forward. "Miles had this idea for a joint venture where he and his scientists wanted to create genetically modified plants that would be drought resistant."

"Given how dry it's been over the past couple of years, especially in South Texas, you can see how valuable that would be if they were successful," Kelsey added.

I nodded. I did see the value. I also knew Miles always had a backdoor plan that centered more around harm than good. As I had no proof other than my past experience with him, I kept my mouth shut.

"He and James Cutter were going to be general partners in the limited partnership they were forming."

"Was James the only investor?" I suspected there were more but hoped Pete would confirm and provide additional details.

He shook his head. "No. Well, he was the only official investor at the time of Miles' death, but a few more had shown interest. That whole part of the deal was a little weird."

"Weird how?"

Pete sipped some more wine. "Mr. Cutter fronted a reasonable amount of cash, but it wasn't going to be enough. That's when Miles started looking for others to help supplement. James got upset and told him if he'd be patient and get things up and running with the money he'd already provided, there would be more to come soon."

"That doesn't make any sense," Kelsey chimed in. "The Cutter family has more than enough to invest whatever Miles needed. Why make him wait?"

Pete shrugged. "I have no idea. I do know Miles was not pleased with the delay, so he reached out to a few more people. We were scheduled to meet today."

"Today, as in less than forty-eight hours after he was found murdered?" I clarified.

Pete nodded. "Yes, which made for a pretty crappy day around the office."

I absorbed his statement in silence as the gears in my brain tried to process the details. "I can only imagine. I'm so sorry." I paused to let the sincerity of my words settle. I truly felt bad for Pete. He'd been working toward being a named partner for quite some time based on what Kelsey had shared. Honestly, I was surprised he hadn't achieved that already given he'd been at the firm for a long time. And despite his questionable behavior at times while not at work, Kelsey always spoke proudly of what he had accomplished.

Figuring it couldn't hurt to ask as the worst he could tell me was no, I forged ahead. "Can you share with me who the other potential investors were?"

Pete leaned back. "If you tell me why you want to know, I might be able to."

"I have no business interest, if that's what you're worried about."

"Then what?"

He wasn't going to let me off the hook on this one. I understood. He needed to protect himself. I figured it couldn't hurt to explain. "One of my old friends who worked with me when we crossed paths with Miles a couple years ago assaulted him the other night and is now being held for questioning regarding his murder."

A low whistle emerged from Pete's pursed lips. "Dang, woman. You never do anything halfway, do you?"

"Pete." Kelsey shot a warning across the room.

"No, he's right. I'm pretty much an all or nothing kinda gal." I smiled and waved off her concern. "Most of my life, that's served me well. Sometimes, not so much." I paused for a moment. "I'm hoping, this time, it will get me some information on others who might have been upset if it turns out Miles had decided to cancel his meeting with the potential investors."

Pete nodded. "I see the angle." He smiled. "It's pretty smart. I respect that."

I returned his smile. "Respect me enough to share the information?"

This time, he laughed. "Sure. None of them are my clients and no official paperwork was drawn up." He learned forward in his chair. "You need to write this down?"

There was no doubt I'd write it down later, but right now, my entire focus was on whatever he was going to say next. "I'm good."

He looked like he was going to say something that would land him in a world of hurt with his wife, who happened to be sitting only a few feet away from him. I'm guessing he felt that vibe, too, as his expression returned to a more serious one. "Okay, here goes. The potential investors were Ted Birmingham, JB Nester, and Karen Bizzy."

Relieved he opted to behave, I thought about those three names. Ted wasn't a big surprise. The Birminghams had more money than they knew what to do with and supported philanthropic projects like the Cutters. Though I didn't think they had any cute catch phrases like Cutter Cares, it wouldn't be a stretch for them to want to invest in something that could make a significant difference in Texas and elsewhere.

Now, JB was another story. He had appeared visibly ill at the forum on Monday night. Guilt over murdering another candidate? I didn't know much about his financial position, but I'd witnessed him trying to climb the social ladder. Being a part of this deal couldn't hurt his progression. If Miles had decided to exclude him, that might have pushed him too far. It seemed a stretch, but possible.

And then, there was Karen. She hadn't seemed upset Sunday night. At least, not until she got a text or email that prompted her to withdraw from the race. I closed my eyes to focus over the past few days. Had I seen her before the forum?

"What are you thinking about, Sadie?" Kelsey's soft voice filtered into my thoughts.

I opened my eyes. I'd almost forgotten there were others in the room. "I'm sorry. I was just processing and trying to see which one of those might be more prone to..." It seemed wrong to finish the sentence.

"You think one of them really killed Miles?" Kelsey's voice held an incredulous tone.

Pete laughed. "That's the whole reason she was grilling me for information, babe."

"If you think that was me grilling you, I need to show you the difference. I don't bring top shelf tequila to people I'm going to grill."

"What would you bring? Just so I know for future reference." Pete chuckled.

It wasn't often I appreciated Pete's sense of humor, but it was a valid question. "The cheap stuff so I could get you drunk quickly, and then you'd talk without me even having to prompt you."

"Good to know." The smile hadn't left his face, so he took it in the spirit it was delivered.

"Maybe you need a walk to clear your head. First thing tomorrow morning," Kelsey suggested. "Get those crazy thoughts out of your head."

"A walk. Yes, walks are good." Then, it hit me. "Karen!"

"Karen what?" Kelsey startled a little at my excitement.

"I saw Karen the same morning Miles was murdered."

Pete sat up straight. "Saw her where?"

"The police had been at my house looking for Dante, and Deputy Matthews had just left. I was still standing on the front steps reeling from everything I'd learned. Then, I saw Karen walking by. But she wasn't her usual self. She seemed distracted, upset even."

"What time was this?"

"Couldn't have been much later than eight."

"Do you know what the time of death was?" Kelsey asked, now fully invested with me in this process.

"Not officially, but Delaney said when the police questioned her, they asked if she heard anything between four and five in the morning. I'm assuming that has to be close."

Kelsey was chewing on her bottom lip. She did that when she was thinking hard. "So, theoretically, she could have killed him and then just walked around aimlessly contemplating her life choices."

Pete laughed at her statement. "I'd say murder is an anti-life choice."

She playfully rolled her eyes at his comment. "Valid point."

"Was she covered in blood or anything?" Pete's eyebrows waggled as he sported a smirk.

"Pete!" Kelsey and I both called him out on that.

"Of course not," I clarified. "But she didn't seem like herself."

As all the information settled around us, Pete was the first to break the silence. "So, Sadie, what are you going to do next?"

I sighed heavily. "I don't know. But I must do something. I can't let my friend be arrested for a crime he didn't commit."

Of course, I didn't continue that statement with the knowledge that freeing Dante could potentially mean Natalie was arrested.

That was a problem for another day.

Chapter Eight

An incessant pounding on the door woke me from a restless sleep. My phone joined the cacophony of noise with incessant buzzing. This week was shaping up to be one for the record books, and not the good kind. I blinked several times to erase the remnants of sleep from my eyes. I had zero desire to get out from under the quilt my nonna in Italy made for me. Here, I was safe and warm. Maybe once all the drama died down, I'd plan a trip to visit her.

I pulled on a robe. I swear, if they broke the door, I was going to file a claim. "Just a minute!" I yelled, hoping to cease the unrelenting banging. I entered the passcode on my phone to stop the buzzing. There was a text message from Jeremy. *Dante has been released.*

Conflicting emotions tumbled in my brain as I made my way to the front door. His release was a good thing, right? They must have finished questioning and found nothing substantial for charges. Of course, this meant they were searching for someone else. Nat, maybe? I would address that problem after I dealt with my early morning visitor. I quickly responded to his text. *Thank you.*

Eventually, I would need to apologize for the things I'd said yesterday. It had been snarky and beneath me. Though doubtful we had any future given the gaping distance between our moral codes, he still deserved not to be on the receiving end of my attitude, even if I was having several bad days in a row.

The pounding picked up, but this time, I was close enough to hear what they were saying. "Open up! Police!"

A quick check of my watch verified it was only about six-thirty. Why in heaven's name would they be at my door this early? It couldn't mean anything good. Before allowing anyone in, a quick check of the feed revealed it was my least favorite law enforcement officer. Because it was him, I decided to have our interaction recorded by the camera so everything that transpired between the deputy and me would be saved on my cloud drive. One could never be too careful.

I opened the door to find him holding a piece of paper tightly in his grasp with his arm stretched out in front of him. Before I could read what it said, his face boasted the smug smirk I'd come to detest. With an exasperated sigh, I asked, "How can I help you this morning, Deputy?"

"Sadie Sabatini, you're under arrest for the murder of Miles Gentry. You have the right to remain silent...

and please do. Anything, and I do mean each and every word you utter from this point while in my custody, can be used against you in a court of law. You have the right to an attorney. If you can't afford an attorney—and let's be honest, we both know you can, but if you feel you can't or don't want to spend your money 'cause you know you're guilty—one will be appointed to you free of charge. Do you understand these rights as they have been read to you?"

He waited for my answer as I stood there in stunned silence. There were a million things I wanted to say or ask, but I knew that would only feed the already massive ego of Deputy Matthews. I understood those rights, even though he took a few creative liberties with them. I just didn't understand why he was reading them to me.

"Hey, do you understand what I just said to you?" Apparently, his patience only extended for a few moments.

"Yes."

He held out the cuffs with so much joy, I would have thought he was giving me a diamond ring or some prized jewel. "Hands behind your back."

He'd been wanting to cuff me since I arrived in town. For whatever reason, something about me irritated him. I hadn't done anything to him, really, except call his bluff when he tried to pull something over on me. I decided I wanted to make sure he was being one hundred percent truthful to me now. "I'd like to see the warrant first."

The joy on his face morphed into irritation. I'd pushed his buttons again, but this time, it wasn't just for fun. I needed to know exactly what was going on. He shoved the paper toward me. "Make it fast."

I skimmed over the document to find the actual charges. I wasn't sure whether to be relieved that the Deputy had, once again, gotten it wrong. The charge was voluntary manslaughter, not murder. It might not seem like much difference, but I'd become familiar enough with the law to know that manslaughter meant a chance for bail. Murder, in ninety-nine point nine percent of circumstances, meant no chance to get out until your trial. I also noted, with relief, there wasn't a charge of tampering with the crime scene. Weird what one found comfort in when things were so very horrible all around you.

"Well? You satisfied?" He held out the cuffs again.

I decided it was better to point out his errors to the chief rather than waste my breath on him. Plus, it would provide him with the opportunity to make corrections. I couldn't have that. I might need this leverage later. I put my hands out in front of me to accept the cuffs, even though they were a tad bit of overkill. It wasn't like I was going to try to escape. That would mean running. And I didn't run.

He clucked his tongue and shook his head. "Nuh, uh. Behind your back."

"Seriously?"

"Does my face look like I'm joking?"

There were so many opportunities for a smart

remark there about his face, but I resisted the temptation. "Can I at least change?"

He finally noticed my attire. The man had roused me from bed. He turned to the other officer with him, a woman I didn't recognize. "You go with her. Make sure she doesn't try nothin' funny."

The woman nodded and followed me inside. I grabbed a sweatsuit and other necessities and headed to the bathroom. "One moment, ma'am."

I waited while she checked my bathroom. She looked to be making sure I didn't have any weapons lying around. I didn't. A mental note was made that the bathroom might make a good hiding place in the future. "Go ahead, but the door stays open."

"Understood." I changed quickly, pulled my hair into a ponytail, and brushed my teeth. Makeup would have to wait.

Returning to my bedroom, I nodded to her. "I'm ready. Thank you for allowing me to change."

She didn't say anything, but nodded. Deputy Matthews could take a few lessons from her. Once back at the front door, I locked it, set the alarm, and turned so he could cuff me. This might be the most humiliated I'd felt in my entire life. I'm certain that was his goal.

The snap of the cuffs sent a ripple of fear down my spine. I'd imagined what would happen if I ever got caught on a job. At least in that scenario, I would have felt justified for going down doing something that made the world a better place. This, right here, was just one horrible mistake.

About ten minutes later, we arrived at the local Sheriff's office. Why it took us ten minutes to get to a place five minutes away was beyond me. My eyes had remained closed to focus on my breathing the entire trip over. The extended trip was probably the pride-filled deputy taking the long way here to give as many people as possible the chance to see me. His version of a victory lap, perhaps?

Thankfully, no one was around when he helped me out of the car. The chief was waiting when we walked in the door. "Here ya go, Chief. Signed, sealed, and delivered as requested."

Chief Seth Parker's presence filled the entire room. His muscles were enough to make a woman swoon without coming across as a beefcake. He worked out, but I couldn't imagine him spending countless hours at a gym lifting weights. His chiseled jaw clenched at his deputy. "Dang it, Jake. Cuffs behind the back, really?"

"She's a murder suspect, boss. Regulations state–"

"I know what the regulations say, Matthews. But she's not a murder suspect." His growl of irritation made me smile, but I managed to keep it on the inside. No sense in distracting these two gentlemen while they worked out their differences.

"Whadda ya mean, Chief?"

He sighed. "The warrant is for manslaughter."

Jake shrugged. "Manslaughter, murder, the end result is the same. Someone is dead because of her."

I lowered my head a bit to hide the small grin I knew was coming out. He wasn't wrong about the end result, but from a legal standpoint, the two charges had significant differences. I knew that. The chief knew that. Deputy Matthews was about to learn.

The chief turned to the bookshelf spanning the back of his office. A moment later, he pulled out a book referred to multiple times if the dog ears and worn look were any indication. "Go sit at your desk and take some time reading the sections on manslaughter and murder. After I speak with Ms. Sabatini, you and I will review the differences. Understood?"

The tone of his voice left room for only one answer, but Jake Matthews obviously wasn't the brightest bulb in the room. "But, sir–"

"Now, Jake."

"Fine. Yes, sir."

Once Jake left, Chief Parker moved behind me and undid the cuffs. Gratitude was my first thought. "Thank you."

"It was by the book, but my Deputy can be a bit overzealous sometimes."

Chief Parker was a follow-the-rules kind of guy. I respected that. "For what it's worth, I tried to get him to cuff my hands in front of me, but he wasn't having it."

He just shook his head. "I don't know what it is about you that puts a burr in his boot, but it certainly makes him act the fool where you're involved."

My shrug hopefully conveyed I was equally

confused. If we were in middle school, I might think he had a crush on me. But grown boys were supposed to have learned better ways to act around the girls. Even the ones they didn't like.

"Let's get you processed, then I'll take your statement."

The next several minutes passed by in a blur as I was fingerprinted, photographed, and then escorted to a room like the one I had met Dante in. Was that just yesterday? It felt like a lifetime had passed. Chief Parker sat down heavily in the chair opposite mine. "Let's get started with the timeline. Where were you Monday morning between the hours of four and five?"

"In bed. Asleep." And before he could ask, I added, "Alone."

"So, no one can verify that?"

I shrugged. I started to offer that there were motion sensor cameras and lights outside my home that recorded when someone entered or left the house, but I realized that might implicate Dante. It also gave me the idea to check those recordings to learn exactly when he left and if Nat was with him or not. "Can I ask you a question?"

One eyebrow raised. "That's not how this works."

Since I knew he wouldn't just let me ask, I decided to throw at least one question in to give him something to think about. "What made them decide to release Dante?"

"You know I can't discuss an ongoing investigation. How you even knew about that detail gives me cause for concern. Did Mr. Miller contact you upon his release? Try to warn you about your impending arrest?"

The question only served to aid my downward spiral. There was a day when Dante would have done just that. Those days were long gone. "I've not heard from Mr. Miller. You can't tell me even if I'm now part of the investigation?"

He chuckled. "Especially because of that."

The man had a point, even if I didn't like it. "Fair enough, I guess."

I continued with the questions. I figured until he insisted I stop, there was no reason not to put them out into the universe. Who knew? Maybe the answers were hiding there. "Why did you arrest me? What proof is there? I should be able to at least ask that." The question had been burning a hole in my head since Deputy Jake showed up at my door.

"Why did you kill Miles Gentry?"

I decided it wasn't in my best interest to be completely cooperative by explaining more than needed. "I didn't."

He sighed and reached into a box on the floor. "Then, how do you explain us finding this knife with his blood on it? And before you suggest otherwise, we checked. It has your fingerprints as well."

For the first time in perhaps a lifetime, I had been rendered speechless twice in one day. It wasn't even ten in the morning yet. That had to be some kind of record.

"Ms. Sabatini? I asked you a question."

Once the initial shock wore off, anger slowly seeped in. "Where did you find that?"

The chief glared. "Exactly where you left it after you killed our victim."

His statement didn't answer my question. Primarily, because neither had I killed Miles nor had I disposed of the alleged murder weapon. It did answer, however, the earlier question I'd asked. Dante was released because they discovered new evidence. Information that implicated me.

I needed some time to process before saying much more. Under normal circumstances, I would have thrown whoever was trying to frame me directly in the path of the oncoming bus. But this wasn't some random stranger who needed to be taught a lesson about dealing with Sadie Sabatini. This was Dante Miller, a long-time friend and team member. The ache in my heart clenched tighter at how far we'd fallen apart.

My emotional trauma could wait. Now, I needed to learn as much as I could before my freedom was completely taken away. Very hard to find the truth inside a six-by-eight-foot cell with nothing but a bed and toilet. It was time to show the chief a bit of the Sabatini sass I'd been known for throughout my life. "I'll repeat again, I didn't kill Miles. I didn't like him. No point in denying that. I had a minor public altercation with him, but that was the end of it. And let's say, just for the sake of your argument, I temporarily lost my marbles and killed him. Why would I have used my own knife, and then, for the love of all that is great in the state of Texas, dispose of it wherever you happened to find it?"

"Sometimes, smart people do stupid things in the heat of passion," he stated with a resigned matter-of-fact tone.

Part of me wanted to explain the only passion I'd ever felt for Miles was disgust and disdain, but my rational side knew that information would not help my case. Instead, I needed to hone in on the timeline they were working with and cast some reasonable doubt on their version of events. "Heat of the moment reactions aren't really my style, but I know there's no way to prove that to you as you haven't known me long enough."

He didn't respond, so I took that as implied permission to continue. "Your theory is Miles and I shared a less than pleasant moment Friday evening at The Club surrounded by a bunch of witnesses. Then, in the middle of the night, I get called down here to your office to bail Dante Miller out of jail. Dante comes home with me and then I sneak *back* out in the wee hours of the morning, taking my butcher knife with me. I get Miles to come out in the woods next to his condo to have a chat. Then, at some point in the aforementioned conversation, I take my knife out, stab him, and discard the murder weapon somewhere nearby. After that I just, what? Go home and return to bed? All before Deputy Matthews comes pounding on my door around seven thirty in the morning looking for Dante, your prime suspect?"

To his credit, his facial expression hadn't changed as I spun my tale of fiction interspersed with a few facts. I had no idea how he could keep a straight face. Even as I laid it all out, the whole scenario resonated as completely preposterous.

"Crimes of passion are rarely logical," he offered after several tense, silence-filled minutes had passed. "I'm obligated to share with you that the Crockett County police are executing a search warrant on your premises while you're in here working on your defense."

This was not good news. I'd stopped worrying about the plastic ring I'd found in the woods. There was no way anyone but me would know that item had been secured from the crime scene, much less point a finger at Natalie. I was more worried they might inadvertently stumble across something from my past, opening a whole new can of bright, shiny trouble for me. I tried to keep all of that hidden away in a cleverly disguised floor safe, but depending on the parameters of the search warrant and how good those people were at their jobs, it was a possibility. "Since you already have the alleged murder weapon, what exactly are you hoping to find?"

"Anything that further connects you with Mr. Gentry. You've already shared you knew him from before. You also knew he'd changed his name. Sounds like you're hiding something, don't you think?"

I was growing weary of this entire conversation. Add to that the fact he'd hit a proverbial nail on the head, it was time I took advantage of my right to remain silent. This went on for a bit until something occurred to me. Miles had been beat up the night before, courtesy of Dante. If the knife had been the murder weapon, shouldn't there have been more blood at the crime scene? Of course, I couldn't ask about that important detail otherwise I'd do their job for them and officially confirm I was there. The fact it was hours after the incident would mean little. So, if it wasn't the beating and most likely not the knife, what—and, more importantly, who—did the killing and why? Another question also formed a heavy stone in the pit of my stomach. If it wasn't the knife that killed him, why would someone go to the trouble to stab him with my knife *after* he was dead? Maybe that could be the crime of passion part?

I decided to make one last effort to cast reasonable doubt without volunteering my internal revelations. "Do you even know what killed him yet? As I recall, that part of the justice wheel doesn't turn too quickly around here."

The entire time I'd been sitting across from this larger-than-life man, I'd kept a close eye on him, studying his body language. He'd kept his face neutral until my last question. Something flickered in his gaze. Something that told me there was more to the story than he was letting on. I decided to go on a fishing expedition with this bait. "You don't know what the cause of death is, do you?"

His gaze hardened. "I'm the one asking the questions here." His steely tone matched his expression.

Before he could say anything further, I cut him off. "Attorney."

It took only a few moments before Chief Parker responded. "Fine. Who is your legal counsel?"

Technically, I didn't have any. I only knew one attorney, so he won the prize. "Pete Jensen."

"You sure about that?"

I was sure he was the only attorney I knew in the greater Wilson or Crockett County area, so he would be a good start. "I'm sure."

"Fine. I'll have you transferred to Crockett County Jail. You can have your one phone call and ask your attorney to meet you there."

"Has bail been set?"

He nodded. "Voluntary manslaughter is one hundred thousand dollars."

If he thought that number would scare me, he was wrong. I knew it translated into ten thousand needed for a surety bond. And even if a cash bond was required, I had that money stored away. I would just need Pete or Kelsey to help me get the funds transferred since I couldn't call on my money gal. One phone call meant just one. That part of the justice system was rarely up for debate. "Cash or bond?"

His head snapped up at my question. "You sure

know a lot about this process for someone who's allegedly so squeaky clean and innocent."

I shrugged. No way was I going to explain to the chief my knowledge of the law had come from years of learning how to circumvent the rules those who served the law had to follow. "I watch a lot of crime dramas on television."

"It's a surety bond."

"Thank you. I'll take that phone call now." Chief Parker pulled out his cellphone and handed it to me. "Seriously?"

He shrugged. "We're a small outfit here. Not like I have a phone in the interrogation room." A quirky smile managed to creep onto his almost always serious face as he gestured around the room. "We don't even really have an interrogation room."

"Fair enough. May I at least have some privacy?"

"I'll be right outside the door."

I nodded. "Understood."

He lifted his tall, muscular frame out of the chair and moved toward the door. "Oh, and Ms. Sabatini?"

"Yes?"

"One phone call only."

I couldn't help myself. I saluted him. "Sir, yes sir."

He shook his head and stepped outside. I immediately dialed Kelsey's number. Thankfully, we'd called each other often enough I had her number memorized. It was probably the only one besides Jeremy's and my parents I could call without having access to my contacts. There was zero point in reaching out to

Jeremy. He would probably deliver a good ol' fashioned *I told you so* before leaving me to rot in jail. Okay, maybe not, but it was too great of a risk.

After a couple rings, Kelsey answered. "Chief Parker? How may I help you?" She was all business, which I found adorable.

"Kelsey, it's me. Sadie."

"Why do you have the chief's cellphone?"

I grinned. "I think the better question is how, or why do you have Chief Parker's cellphone number saved in your phone?"

"Don't you worry about that." I could almost imagine the smile on her face and the twinkle in her eye at having a secret. No worries, I was confident in my ability to get her to spill the details once all of this was over.

"We'll cover that later. Right now, I need you to call Pete and have him meet me at the Crockett County Jail."

"Oh no, Sadie! What's happened?"

"I promise I'll explain later. I don't know how much time the chief is going to give me. I'm being transferred and processed for voluntary manslaughter."

"For what? Oh my! This is not good."

I shook my head. "No, it most definitely is not. I need Pete to be there so I can arrange bail and get a court date set. Once released, I can figure out who really did this."

There was a pause, a little longer than I would

have liked. "You do know Pete isn't a criminal attorney, right? How much is the bail?"

"I know, but if I really end up needing one, he probably knows more people in that realm than I do."

"Okay, I'll call him right now and have him meet you."

"Thanks, Kelsey. I owe you one, maybe two for this."

"How much is bail?"

I answered her question without even thinking. "One hundred thousand. Surety bond."

"Okay. Be careful, Sadie."

I would typically respond to her that I always am, but the fact I'd just been arrested suggested otherwise. "I'll try."

I disconnected the call and deleted the number from the history. No sense in giving him any reason to reach out to Kelsey and involve her any more than I already had. I knocked on the door. "I'm finished and ready to go."

Ironically, what worried me most in the present was that Chief Parker might assign the eager Deputy Matthews to escort me to the Crockett County Jail. Thankfully, there was a uniformed officer, apparently from the county, who had been summoned for the transport.

As he helped me into the back of the car, I caught movement out of the corner of my eye. Across the street, leaning up against a light pole, stood Dante and

Natalie. His expression was one of sorrow and concern. Hers, on the other hand, resembled pure joy.

In that moment, I knew, somehow, she'd set me up.

Chapter Nine

Thankfully, the officer didn't attempt conversation on the thirty-minute ride to the jail. Though, I guess when you think about it, he only knew me as a suspected murderer. Or was it a suspected man slaughterer? Was that even an official term? Regardless, I had more than enough time to think about why Natalie was so happy to see me arrested. I put aside all the emotions tumbling around in my brain and my gut. They weren't going anywhere. I added them to the list of things to be dealt with later. Right now, I needed to think straight.

They had found a knife–apparently, *my* knife with Miles' blood on it. There was no surprise that my fingerprints or DNA were on the knife. It was missing from the kitchen.

Wait.

Mine was *missing* from the kitchen! I took some calming breaths to focus on exactly when I'd realized it was gone. The stone sitting in my stomach tripled in size as the details rushed forward. It was the day after I'd bailed Dante out of jail. After the night I'd welcomed him into my home.

Sadness settled heavily into every pore of my body, filling my heart with pain. There was no other explanation my brain could muster. Dante had taken the knife. He'd either used it on Miles, or Natalie had. Were they so angry over the team splitting up, they believed this was necessary? Framing me for murder or manslaughter certainly qualified as a vengeful act. Or was there something more to their plan? Had Dante been filled with such hate for Miles that he saw the knife and hunted him down to kill him? Chief Parker mentioned a crime of passion. That series of events didn't fit with the man I'd known Dante to be. But people changed, right? The good Lord knew I'd certainly been trying.

I needed some sleep or maybe wine to outline all the possible conclusions. Since it was doubtful either of those would be available in the immediate future, I opted to close my eyes and avoid my current reality. Instead, I focused on trying to survive one of the worst days of my life.

Thirty minutes later, I'd been delivered to the prisoner intake section of the jail and my good ol' friend, Agnes, met me with a frown. "What in tarnation are you doing here? In cuffs, no less?"

My smile was weak because, oddly enough, seeing a familiar and almost sympathetic face right now helped center me. "Really bad case of girl gets framed.

I'm sure you've heard the story before." I didn't expect her to believe my claim of innocence. I'm certain everyone who came through those doors said something similar.

She nodded and led me into an interrogation room. The cuffs were attached to a metal bar on my side of the table. This further reinforced the notion that Dante had only been brought in for questioning rather than on any official charges. He hadn't been wearing the silver bracelets when I'd been here with him.

"Can I get you something to drink while we do the paperwork, and you wait for your attorney?"

As I'd missed my morning coffee thanks to all the commotion, I nodded. "May I have some coffee, please?"

"Sure thing. Cream or sugar?"

"No, thank you."

"Be back in a minute."

While I waited for Agnes, I focused on the next steps. Pete was going to arrive soon, and bail would be arranged. First order of business, after a hot shower and nap, was to find Dante and Natalie. I also wanted to check out the facility where Miles' business was conducted. There had to be a lab somewhere with incriminating evidence. Finding that might be easier than my former teammates.

A few minutes later, Agnes was back with a steaming cup of coffee. After a tentative sip, I had to admit it wasn't half bad. While not the cappuccino I was used to, as brewed coffees go, it wasn't the worst I'd had, either. "Thank you. This was even better than I expected."

She leaned in and winked. "I might have secured yours from the officers' break room. They always get the good stuff."

Despite everything, I smiled. Both at her attempt to humor me along with the better version of coffee than visitors and inmates typically received. "Then, I extend an extra measure of gratitude to you for your kindness."

Agnes shrugged. "I told you before. I see a lot of folks come through here. Some evil, some bad, some wrong place, wrong time, and on occasion, those who are caught in the middle of something bigger than they can handle."

"Which one do you think I am?" I hoped it wasn't one of the first two. Surely, she wouldn't get the good coffee for someone she categorized as bad or evil, would she?

Taking out her pen and the clipboard with the paperwork, her gray gaze settled on me. "I think you're caught up in the middle of something bigger than you know how to handle."

With a sigh, I merely nodded. When the woman was right, she was spot-on right. "Let's get started."

All business now, Agnes asked me the requisite questions, which I answered truthfully and without hesitation. Chief Parker could take some interrogation lessons from her. Rule number one: Always butter the suspect up with decent coffee. That rule was especially important when you arrested someone first thing in the morning before their alarm had even gone off.

Paperwork complete, Agnes left me to my own devices for several minutes before Pete was ushered in. He waited for the officer to close the door and leaned forward. "You wanna tell me what in the heck happened?"

"Would you believe me if I said I was being framed?" Even as the words left my mouth, I knew how lame it sounded. Criminals, guilty ones, claimed this kind of stuff all the time. They ruined it for those of us who really were innocent.

"At the end of the day, it doesn't matter. Innocent or guilty, the firm will provide the best representation possible for you."

Wow. I didn't expect that, and honestly, I wasn't sure how to feel. He was a straight shooter, I'd give him that. Right now, I didn't have the energy to defend myself, so I moved forward. "What's next?"

"Your bail is currently being processed. You'll be given a court date. They will give you a set of rules to follow while out on bail. And for the love of all that's good in the state of Texas, show up at the hearing and don't get into any more trouble."

While I'd heard all that he said, I focused on the first part. "What do you mean my bail is being processed? I haven't even asked you to arrange the money transfer to pay for it."

"Because my wife is posting your bail."

I stood up quickly. Well, as much as I could cuffed

to the table. "Pete, that's not necessary. I have the money. I only had one phone call and you were it."

He narrowed his gaze. "Technically, my wife was your one phone call. You know how she can be. I'm picking up guilty vibes from her about something. But since men, or at least this man, has given up trying to figure his wife out, I know she has her reasons. At the end of the day, that's good enough for me. It also doesn't hurt she's one hundred percent convinced of your innocence."

"But you're not?" My words bordered more accusatory than I'd wanted, but I didn't like his implication.

"Sadie, please. Sit down."

Because his tone had become softer, I complied, even though I was still hurt. "Fine."

He leaned forward. "Look, as a lawyer, I have to keep my emotions and feelings out of it. Otherwise, I could do something stupid and jeopardize a case." A faraway look crossed his gaze. "There's a reason I don't do criminal law anymore."

I really wanted to know what happened, but this was neither the time nor place. "Maybe some time you can tell me the story. Until then, I'm going to pretend you think I'm innocent, but believe it's in my best interest for you not to show me. Deal?"

"Deal."

Agnes stepped in before our conversation could continue. "Bail has been posted. Just a few more papers to sign and you'll be able to leave."

I noticed she didn't say free to go. I might be allowed to leave this building, but until my innocence was proven, free wasn't a word anyone would mention when I came up as a topic of conversation. And, rest assured, people were going to talk.

The paperwork was completed in short order, and I sat on a bench as a police officer fitted me with a brand-new piece of jewelry: an ankle bracelet. It most certainly did not match my outfit, but it was better than being dressed in orange, even if it was the new black according to an old television show.

"All right, ma'am, this bracelet monitors your whereabouts. If you are outside the county limits for more than thirty minutes, we will get an alert. We'll track your location and then arrest you for violation of your parole. Understood?"

"Yes." I didn't like it, but I understood. "Is it waterproof?"

"Yes, ma'am, up to fifty feet. No hot tub, though."

"Lucky for me, I guess, that I don't own one. Thank you."

"Ma'am."

The officer finished connecting it, then left me alone until Pete and Kelsey arrived. Pete stood by the door while Kelsey sat next to me, pulling me in her comforting embrace. "Everything is going to be all right. I know it."

Words wouldn't form, so I simply nodded. Thankfully, she must have understood my distress. "Pete, why don't you get the car? I'll get Sadie out there so we can go home."

"You got it, babe."

Once Pete left, I turned my head so I could look at her. Her beautiful cherub face sported the smallest hint of a smile. Her eyes, which normally sparkled while sharing a small bit of the joy she brought to everyone around her, held a hint of trouble. Pete was right. There was something she felt guilty about. "Are you okay?"

My question caught her off guard. "I'm fine. I'm not the one who was arrested. You poor thing, you must be so traumatized."

It had been a traumatic experience, but I also knew my friend. She was not fine. "It's not been my best day. Because of that, I will keep my questions about what's going on with you at bay for now."

"It's nothing." She waved away my concern. "Sometimes we regret our actions and hurt those around us, even if they aren't aware."

Was she talking about my situation now or hers? I certainly regretted the choices I'd made when carrying out the job against Miles. In retrospect, they certainly had not played out the way I'd wanted. If they had, he would still be alive. He might have been in jail, but he wouldn't currently be laying in the morgue. "Sometimes, we simply do the best we can and hope for a positive outcome."

She nodded, but I wasn't sure it was from agreement. She put her arm around my shoulders. "Come on, Sadie. Let's blow this popsicle stand."

She was right. This wasn't the time or place to hash all of this out. Pete had said she believed in my innocence. For today, that was enough. "I can't blow it up as I'm certain that is a violation of my probation, but let's get the heck out of here."

We stood and made our way out the same door I'd arrived through. Time had lost all meaning today. Thankfully, we were exiting from a door hidden from view of the main parking lot and, more importantly, from the building Jeremy worked in. I had no idea if he was in the office, out on patrol, or maybe had this time off. It wasn't like we were sharing in each other's lives now. Oh well, it was for the best. I needed to focus on clearing my name and finding the real killer.

The ride back to Wilson was cloaked in the same silence as my trip to the county jail. I tried to focus, but truthfully, all I wanted was a nap. Rest did wonders for mental capacity. And the good Lord knew I needed all the brain power I could harness.

Using the app on my phone to open the garage door as we pulled into the driveway, I waited for Pete to stop the car. I reached to the front seat and squeezed Kelsey's shoulder. "Thank you for everything. There aren't words to properly express how much I appreciate both of you. I'm going to arrange for the funds to be transferred to an account that I can then use to pay you back for the bail."

Before I could say anything further, Kelsey shook

her head. "Absolutely not." She unhooked her seatbelt and turned. "You will use all those super-secret spy skills from your past to find the real killer. In the meantime, you show up at any scheduled hearings, don't violate the conditions of your parole, and everything will be set right again. We'll have our money, you'll have your freedom. Easy peasy lemon squeezy."

"With liberty and justice for all." I finished her passionate speech by adding a small smile. She had to have been a cheerleader in high school.

She nodded and I even caught a glimpse of a grin on Pete's face in the rearview mirror. He added, "All right, ladies, I need to get Kelsey back to work along with taking care of your case file and briefing the attorney handling your representation."

"Thanks again. I truly appreciate all you've done for me today. I won't forget it." Before I exited, I decided to add one more thing. "And Kelsey, I don't know if you were talking about my situation earlier or something going on with you when you mentioned regretting your actions, but despite everything going on in my life right now, I'm still your friend. I'm here for you if you need to talk."

Tears glistened in her gaze. "Don't you worry about me. I'm a big girl and I intend to fix my wrongs, and then everything will be okay for both of us."

Her statement made zero sense, so I just nodded. "Okay, but the offer still stands."

"Thank you."

Regardless, I planned to allocate some brainpower

to figuring out whatever she had going on. I owed her that. If she was troubled, I wanted to help. "I've got your back. Now and always."

Before Kelsey could answer, Pete jumped in. "As much as I hate to interrupt this moment between you two, we all have things we need to be about this afternoon."

He was right. "Understood. Thank you both again for your help."

Their car pulled away and took with it a reasonable measure of the optimism Kelsey had inspired. I knew I was innocent, but proving it was another matter. Despite my desire for rest, I decided a walk to clear my head and organize the tumbling thoughts would be necessary before that happened.

I went into the house and noted, with some appreciation, the search had been done with reasonable care. Only a few things were out of place. After returning them, I checked the status of the safes. None appeared to be disturbed, but I opened and double checked the contents just in case Nat had decided to pay a visit while I was away. Thankfully, my fake IDs, travel cash, and other tools of the trade were still in place.

Since I was already in warm clothes, no wardrobe change was required to ward off the slight chill in the air. Thanks to the cooler temperatures, my baggy sweats would hide my new jewelry courtesy of the Crockett County Sheriff's Department. Long pants would be my wardrobe choice for the foreseeable future. This adornment would certainly clash with anything I sold at Tesoro.

Thinking of my shop made me miss being there today. I always enjoyed visiting with the locals who frequented it. If word got out about my arrest, I wasn't sure my bottom line would survive this hit to my reputation. Maybe I should call my sister to see if she could fix this and spin my way out of this mess. On second thought, that would mean my parents would find out. I couldn't have that.

I set out at a brisk pace, unsure of where my steps would take me, just knowing I needed to take them. As if of their own will, they led me to the entrance of the RV park tucked away at the end of the peninsula that comprised Wilson. This little area continued to be a source of much debate amongst the Wilsonites. For whatever reason, the original developers had carved out this small section of land, right on the lake, and not incorporated it into the boundary lines of the town. Which meant the people who lived here were not subject to the rules, regulations, and deed restrictions of the town. They also were not allowed to vote for board members or take advantage of resident-only amenities. Neither of which seemed to bother them.

EZ was one of the folks who lived here. She, however, also had property in Wilson proper. As such, she got the best of both worlds. Speaking of EZ, I caught a glimpse of her sitting in one of the Adirondack chairs on the dock smoking a cigarette. Walking up to the other chair, I pointed. "Is this seat taken?"

"It's a free country." Then, she smiled. "Although, guess not technically for you at the moment."

I knew she was teasing, but it still stung a little. She noticed the look on my face. "Too soon?"

"Definitely too soon." I took a seat and ran my hand over the beautiful wood. "These are new, aren't they?" The last time I'd been over this way, one either had to stand or sit directly on the dock.

"Yup, bought them last week. Figured if I was gonna smoke out here to enjoy the view, I'd make myself comfortable."

"Nice choice."

We sat in silence for a few minutes before EZ snuffed out her cigarette and turned toward me. "You know, I've never been friends with a criminal before."

"Alleged criminal," I corrected with more than a little irritation in my tone. "This is America. We're innocent until proven guilty."

She laughed, which sent her into a coughing fit. "You really should lay off those things," I shared, pointing to the pack of cigarettes sitting on the arm of her chair.

"You have bigger things to worry about, don't you?" As if to prove her point, she took another one out of the pack, tapped it on the chair, and lit up. After a long drag, she added, "And innocent until proven guilty isn't how the court of public opinion works."

She was aggravatingly accurate. I, however, wasn't going to give her the satisfaction of admitting that detail. Something in her words inspired me, though. I knew this was a grave miscarriage of justice, but I'd been dealing with these types of situations for well over a decade, some might even say my whole life. In school, I ensured those who had been wronged would be made whole. The only difference this time was that I was the client. If I could figure out a way to help others, I should be able to find a way to help myself, right?

Once I'd cemented that conviction in my brain, I looked at EZ, who was calmly enjoying her stress release activity. "Tell me something to take my mind off all of this. It will still be waiting for me, but I need a distraction."

After a moment, she let the smoke out of her mouth in perfect little circles. She'd obviously practiced that a lot. "You see or hear about the flyers circulating all over town?"

"The smear campaign against Alan, right?" It was possible there had been other flyers going around I'd missed while away dealing with personal matters.

"The very one."

"Yes, Denise stopped by my shop to give me the four-one-one. Of course, her version was colored with anger and righteous indignation."

EZ laughed. "She's a feisty one, all right. But I like that about her."

"Me too."

"I'm guessing Ted underestimated her interest in Alan."

This grabbed my attention. I turned my focus from the lake to EZ. "Wait. What? The nearly Mr. Perfect

Ted Birmingham was behind all of this? The heir apparent and perfect son of the Birmingham dynasty?"

Her deep laugh elicited another cough. She reached beside her chair and lifted an insulated cup to her mouth. It most likely wasn't water. Either way, I didn't care. She obviously had good gossip on this one. Right now, someone else's issues were a welcome change.

She shook her head. "Not directly, no. He would never do something so obvious."

"Then, I'm confused."

"There's a woman who serves on the committee that manages the community social media. You know, information that gets shared with all the people here in Wilson."

"So, the information hub?"

"Other than the unofficial rumor mill, yes."

"How did she come into this juicy bit of knowledge? Since the voting on the RV park utilities happened before it even officially came into being. That's a long time to hold on to such important knowledge, and the timing is pretty suspect. Did Ted just reveal this information to her?" I still had a hard time thinking Ted would betray a confidence like that, but then again, I was dealing with some potentially serious betrayal myself, so anything was possible.

EZ puffed on her cigarette a few more times before answering. "Nah, he's not the type. She probably had her ear to the door and overheard Ted and Robert talking about the election. Being aware of the feud between the Birminghams and the Knightly family, it's not a big leap for her to understand the last thing they wanted would be for him to be on the board for another couple years. Nothing but a skip and a little jump from there for her to take matters into her own hands."

This series of statements caught my attention, and I sat up straighter in the chair. "Did she make it all up, or did Alan really vote against the RV park?" Even though I knew Alan typically opposed anything Ted supported, this seemed far reaching. Everyone knew how much we all benefited from allowing utilities here in the park. It would be better for the environment, the smell, and the lake.

After another sip, she smiled. "Oh, this woman would get a Pulitzer Prize for creative fiction."

"Seriously?"

"Seriously."

"Wow! I'm learning that local politics are far more intense than I'd anticipated." I'd seen my fair share of people playing dirty over the years, but I'd not gotten the impression that politics in Wilson played such a powerful role. I would need to pay more attention going forward. *If I wasn't in jail, that is.*

"I don't think this had anything to do with political power. Age old lust, baby. That's what was going down here."

That made more sense. Ted's wife was out of the picture, at least for now, which made him a prime target for status climbing socialites wanting to draw the attention of powerful men. This woman had to be playing the long game, though. Ted might be a future person of influence as the heir apparent, but presently he was nothing more than a token chess piece for his father as far as I'd observed.

Since we were on the subject of local politics, I wanted her take on the events the night of the forum. "You have any explanations for the odd behavior of JB and Karen on Sunday night?"

"Besides being ecstatic Ms. Bizzy Body withdrew from the race?"

"That, and the fact that JB looked like death warmed over."

"Sick would be my guess." She shrugged as though it had no meaning. Of course, she didn't know what I did. Both Karen and JB were potential investors in Miles' business. The forum was literally the night after he was found murdered. I thought back to Ted. Had he been acting odd? Nothing had been out of character that I could remember or had observed.

"I don't think he was physically ill." It was just a hunch, but I felt strongly about it.

"Why do you care?"

"Just odd that out of the seven running for those open spots, one was murdered, one withdrew from the race, and another looked like he'd rather be any place but there. Feels like something else is at play to me. Don't you think?"

When she didn't answer, I decided to let those thoughts simmer in my head and return to her early sharing. "Do you think lust played a role in Miles' death?"

"What?"

"You said earlier you didn't think the woman helping Ted out had any desire for power, just wanted his attention and affection."

She laughed at my statement. I'm glad she found me so funny today. "Oh, I think she wants more than affection. She wanted him to dip a chip into her salsa, if you know what I mean."

Eww. I knew what she meant, but there were at least a thousand other less nasty ways she could have said it. "Is that a Texas euphemism?" I asked as her merriment continued. Maybe I should quit my day job and become a stand-up comedian.

"No, just one I made up. Making the boys at the club laugh when they get a little more handsy than I'd like is the best way to get them to stop and still tip big."

"Whatever works, I guess." I tried not to think about EZ fending off men who wanted more than a dance. It had to be exhausting. Which made me wonder why she still did it. Wanting to direct her back to my original question, I asked, "Now that we've established your knack for witty phrases, can we get back to the subject of Miles and your thoughts about a possible motive for murder?"

She nodded, but she finished her cigarette before answering. Though I was impatient for her response, it never served me well to push EZ into revealing anything. Instead, I stared out at the lake and tried to soak up some of its calm as I waited.

"I'm not sure if it was lust or not, but something odd happened Friday night into early Saturday morning around here."

"Such as?"

"I was coming home from work in the wee hours of the morning."

How anyone could stay out, much less work, that late–or was it early?–baffled me. Apparently, men had no issue keeping odd hours for the entertainment The Foxy Lady provided. "What time do you normally get off on the weekend?"

"Typically around five or five-thirty in the morning."

With the mention of the time, my brain went into a red alert. "You didn't see anything at the condos by the golf course on your way home, did you?" The timing matched the estimated window of Miles' death.

"No, I didn't notice anything, but gotta admit, I'm not really looking for anything but the chance to unwind and get some shut-eye."

Without thinking, I shared, "I don't know how you can keep doing that at your age."

"Hey, watch it or you'll leave here not any smarter than when you arrived."

Though I'd meant it in a teasing way, my words must have struck a chord of pain somewhere in her psyche. I reached over and put my hand on her fore-arm. "I meant no offense, just an observation that I can barely stay up past midnight these days, so I can't imagine working until four or five in the morning."

"You get used to it," she admitted. "Besides, sleep is for the weak. Caffeine and cigarettes, baby. That's all the go juice needed for most days."

"I would be lost without caffeine as well. I really am sorry."

She waved my apology off. "If that's the worst thing said to me today, it won't be a half-bad day."

Part of me wanted to ask why she still worked there. She'd recently inherited more than enough money to not have to work, but she obviously still showed up. As I considered the "special" relationship she shared with Robert Birmingham, I thought perhaps as long as he was a patron of The Foxy Lady, EZ would keep her job. Knowing there was no sense in pursuing that line of questioning with her, I prompted, "You were saying you saw something odd on your way home."

EZ nodded. "Well, you know how buddy-buddy I am with Richard and Karen Bizzy, right?"

This time, it was her making me laugh, which ended in a very unladylike snort. "Oh yes, the very best of friends, as I recall. If by friends, you mean mortal enemies."

A small smile curved at the corner of her weathered lips. It was no secret there was no love lost between the Bizzys and EZ. Their feud might not be as old as the Knightly and Birmingham one, but it was just as powerful. "Mortal enemies might be a bit of a stretch. Sworn enemies, for sure."

I wasn't sure there was a difference. "To-may-to, ta-mah-to. Either way, you're enemies. So spill!"

"Okay, okay. Relax. You act like you're out on bail or something. Oh wait!"

"Ha, ha, very funny. Are we going to debate the difference between sworn and mortal enemies, or are you going to tell me what you saw? As you mentioned, I don't have all the time in the world. My preliminary hearing is on Friday, so tick-tock." Though said with some humor, the underlying message was clear. I needed answers, and I needed them fast.

Her smile faded. "Okay, okay. Sorry. But they started it."

"What are you, ten years old?" I teased, trying to make her smile again.

She twirled her finger through the pigtail closest to me and offered a not-so-innocent grin. "Sometimes."

I had no one to blame but myself for her sassy response. I chuckled and prompted her to continue. "You were saying?"

A victorious smile appeared. I'd let her have this one if I could just get some more information. "Anyway, I'm mindin' my own business on my way home, and the Bizzy fortress was lit up like a Christmas tree. The mister and missus were standing in the driveway arguing."

"At five or six in the morning?"

"Closer to six. So, being the good neighbor and

concerned citizen, I stopped, rolled down the window, and told them they needed to bring it down a few notches or I would be forced to call the cops *and* report them to the HOA."

Her last threat was highly entertaining since everyone knew Karen was the person responsible for delivering warnings and citations to residents when complaints came into the Homeowner's Association. "And how did they respond?"

Instead of answering me right away, EZ pulled out another cigarette and went through her routine before lighting it up. After a few draws and puffs, all of which I endured with a patience I didn't think I possessed, she leaned toward me. I met her in the middle, anxious to hear whatever she was going to share.

"Before I tell you, I need you to know all I have is the *what* and not the *why*. I happen to know you are like a dog with a bone when it comes to stuff like this."

I tried to feign hurt, but she was right. Though, I wasn't going to openly admit it. "Fine. You tell me the *what* and I'll get to the bottom of the *why*." Unless, of course, I learned early on it was not related to Miles' murder. Then, to be honest, what the Bizzys did at any time of the night or day was not my business and I truly didn't care. I only stuck my nose in other people's affairs when it served my clients or, in this instance, myself.

EZ leaned back in her chair, apparently satisfied with my response, and stared out at the lake. Finally, she opened her mouth. "Richard's hands had blood all over them."

Chapter Ten

I had no response to EZ's revelation. There was no sense in asking follow-up questions as she'd already warned she didn't know why. And, of course, that would have been my next question. Instead, I spent a few more moments looking out at the lake before standing. "Thank you for telling me. I have no idea if it means anything significant, but knowledge is power, so I appreciate you sharing some of yours with me."

She glanced in my direction. "Be careful, Sadie."

The time for being careful had long passed. "See you later, EZ."

"Later."

My feet guided me on the route to my home while my brain tried to assemble the bits of information I'd been accumulating. I would need to write them down soon to learn possible connections between all this randomness.

A thought swept across my overworked brain. I recalled Karen had been walking aimlessly down the street in front of my house the morning of Miles' death. Had Richard somehow been involved? If so, why or how? Had Karen been worried her quiet husband of few words was capable of murder? The timeline made it a possibility. Maybe Richard had confronted Miles for some reason. When Karen learned about that, she what? Finished him off? I sighed. The logic didn't work here, and out of the two of them, I would have pegged Karen as the more likely suspect.

Karen was, according to Pete, a potential investor. The only reason I could think she might possibly want Miles dead was if he'd turned down her money. But knowing Miles as I did—or had—that didn't seem likely, either. Which brought me right back to the *why* yet again.

Instead of going home, I turned toward the marina. Even though I had a boat slip at the back of my property, I also rented a spot at the Wilson Marina. It was always good to have multiple avenues of escape. You never knew when one of them might come in handy. Right now, the only thing I wanted to escape from was the craziness of this day.

I walked past Jackie's Ship Store and the office where Lester would typically be if he wasn't out on the docks doing whatever it was he did or didn't do. Given the state of disrepair many of the boat slips displayed, it was my opinion he didn't spend as much time out here as he should. I used my key card to open the magnetic lock, allowing access to the leased slips. My boat was in the last row, closest to the lake's entrance. Again, for quick escape reasons. There was a bonus that those slips, because they were older and the farthest away, came at a discounted price.

The boat purred to life, and I maneuvered it out of the marina and through the no-wake zone. Once in the clear, I pushed the throttle down and felt the engines roar to life under me. Exhilaration filled every pore as I sped over the glassy water. The wind whipped through my hair, and I felt truly alive for the first time in days.

After ten or fifteen minutes of adrenaline rush, I slowed the engine and directed the boat to the center of the lake, facing west. This was the best seat in the house to witness sunset. I never tired of watching the sky turn to beautiful shades of orange, sometimes laced with muted reds or purples. Truly a sight to behold. Breathing slowly in and out, I let the peace of nature and the beauty of this magnificent daily sight calm my soul. Though no closer to any solutions for my current situation, all the frenzied activity inside my brain calmed and provided a sense of peace, even if only temporary.

Once the sun disappeared, I turned on the required lights and headed to the marina. Jackie's store still had its lights on, even though their hours of operation for the day had ended. I could hear raised voices despite being several feet away. Curious, I moved in the relative darkness and positioned myself next to a window where the conversation was better heard.

"I can't believe you! How could you even think about going into business with that man? You didn't think."

I'd have recognized that voice anywhere. Lester Price. Though he didn't specify which man, it wasn't far-fetched to believe he was referring to Miles. Pete hadn't mentioned Jackie as a potential investor, but she might have been a last-minute addition if one of the other investors backed out. Maybe Jackie had approached him, and he told Karen he didn't need her money? Or, if James Cutter got cold feet, Miles would have had to raise a lot of capital for his venture. I'd need to ask Pete about that later. Right now, I wanted to hear more of this conversation.

"I was getting to know him, nothing more. You just can't stay out of my business, can you? Every time you get involved, bad things happen."

That was an interesting tidbit Jackie shared. It made me wonder what other bad things had happened.

"I would think you'd be a little more grateful!"

"If you think this makes up for the past, you're wrong. If just once, Lester, you would think through things with your pea-sized brain, you'd realize all this does is put me at risk...again! You never stop to think how your actions might affect others."

I had no idea what they were talking about, but this was one soap opera I didn't want to miss. Focusing on someone else's problems made me worry less about mine.

"Seems to me this time you came out smelling like roses, even if I didn't plan for that to happen. You're getting support for your spot on the board, little sis. If you think that was part of any plan of mine, you're wrong."

I heard a hollow laugh before Jackie responded. "You really are an idiot if you think that offer of support was real. Can't you see what her game plan is? Of course not! You never look past the obvious, which explains, in part, why you got the crap beat out of you."

I hated that I wouldn't get to see a beat-up Lester. Couldn't have happened to a better guy.

"How was I to know one-word Richard was such a hot head?"

"Because the strong silent types often are. Ugh, you don't know the first thing about people."

Well, that might be a partial answer to EZ's *why* equation. Richard did a number on Lester. Was Lester behind Karen backing out of the election? That might explain the beating, but not Karen lending her support to Jackie. Since Jackie thought it was obvious for Lester to know, he possessed knowledge I didn't.

"I know I didn't deserve for him to wail on me like that," Lester whined.

"That's because you never think past what's right in front of you and everyone else pays the price. Instead of trying to make up for the past, you screwed up again. Just stop sticking your nose in my business. Nothing you can do will ever change what happened. And you wonder why people don't respect you!"

The strong desire to laugh out loud at Jackie's statement required me to stifle that impulse. Lester? Respected? Not in this lifetime.

"You worry too much. My choices protect you, even if you don't appreciate it at the time."

"Big brother knows best, right? That's such BS. All I wanted was to talk to Miles to gain information I could use against him in the election."

There were a few moments of silence. Maybe Lester was thinking about that possibility now? Finally, his voice filtered through the window again. "Why do you think I did what I did? I was trying to protect you. One of your competitors has backed out, thanks to me, and another is dead. I'd say that greatly increases your chances. You're welcome!"

Something in the way he made those statements—cold and calculating—sent shivers down my spine. He hadn't added 'thanks to me' for the competitor being dead, but not even Lester was stupid enough to admit to murder out loud. It also sounded like he had somehow got Karen to drop out of the race. Something from her past? While I hadn't thought Lester had it in him to kill, his recent statements made me think twice about that assumption. Had all of this been about something from the past, the local election, or just an odd coincidence? And now my head was hurting again. How annoying.

"I didn't want your so-called help then, and I sure as heck don't need it now."

"You and I both know that's not true, little sister. I'm keeping you safe."

"Get out!"

The sound of footsteps forced me further into the shadows. The door opened, then slammed shut. Lester yelled, "You could have just said thank you!"

I peeked around the corner of the building to see him stomping off toward his houseboat. After a moment, loud music from that area filled the night air. I figured it best to get moving now before Jackie came out and discovered me being nosey.

I hurried past the ship store and office. During the walk home, the words Jackie said kept circling in my brain to find deeper meaning. If she was telling Lester the truth, and that was a big if, she confirmed investing wasn't her goal. She only talked up Miles to discredit him later. Ha! She should have just asked me. I could have supplied her with more than enough intel on Miles. Heck, I might have even been willing to discredit him for her. None of that explained why Richard would beat up Lester. Make no mistake, I had no real issue with him doing so, I just wanted to understand why. Did these dots connect somehow and lead to Miles and his death?

More questions. No answers. No time like the present to try and get information that would wrap up at least a few of those dangling threads. Instead of home, my feet turned me back toward the RV park.

Richard and Karen Bizzy lived right across the street from there, a source of much angst for the couple. Their desire to rid their community of the nuisance neighbors–their words, not mine–was well known throughout the town.

As I walked up to their front door, I checked the time. A little after seven, so not too late to make a neighborly visit. I rang the doorbell and reminded myself in the middle of my mental pep talk there were weapons on the premises, a little lesson I'd learned during a previous visit to their home. I inhaled and exhaled slowly to keep myself in the right frame of mind. Information was needed; a trip to the hospital on a stretcher, or worse, a body bag, was not the goal. When I finally did make it home tonight, I planned to reward myself with a glass of wine, maybe two.

Color me surprised when Richard answered the door. "Hey."

"Hi, Richard. May I come in?"

Though he looked a little surprised to see me, he nodded. "Sure."

Once inside, I followed him into the living room. He gestured toward the sofa. "Drink?"

"Yes, please."

"Wine?"

"That would be wonderful." My lips curled in a slight smile. Not just at the thought of wine, but the fact he'd still managed this entire conversation with only one word at a time. He was a master of this for sure.

"Red?"

"Please." I studied him as he poured the wine. He had a solid build–not heavy, but not thin, and dark brown hair, cut short but long enough to still require him to brush it every day to keep it in line. A whisper of white peeked out from the dark strands. Muscled, but not overly so. He was a quiet man, by all accounts. I don't think anyone had ever witnessed him speak more than a single word at any given time. Guess he'd learned early on Karen did enough talking for them both. Whatever their arrangement, it worked for them. Far better than any I'd ever had. Given the current state of my relationship with Jeremy, better than I could reasonably expect in the future as well.

He handed me the wine, and I noticed the scrapes and bruises on his hand. I did my best to act shocked. "Richard! What happened to your hands?"

"Nothing."

"Doesn't appear to be nothing. Are you all right?"

"Yup."

And the trend continued. I raised my non-wine-holding hand. "My apologies. It's none of my business. Thank you for the wine."

"Yup."

Without another word, he moved toward the hallway leading to another part of the house. "Company."

"Be right there. Thanks, dear."

"Yup."

I'd only managed a couple sips when Karen

entered the room. The moment she saw me, she stopped. An incredulous look crossed her face, followed by what resembled anger. I didn't expect her to be happy to see me. Not that I blamed her. We never seemed to come down on the same side of, well, anything.

"What in the blue bonnet blazes are you doing here? Come to extort something else from me? I dropped out of the race. What more do you want?"

She couldn't have shocked me more if she'd slapped me. Truthfully, I might have preferred it to hearing one more thing that didn't make any sense today. From what I overheard, I'd assumed Lester was the one who got her to drop out of the race. Now, I doubted my interpretation of the argument. "What in heaven's name are you talking about?"

Karen moved to the bar area, grabbed her phone, and swiped a few times before shoving the screen up to my face. After I stepped back a bit to see whatever had her so riled up, I focused on the large letters. There, in black and white and a font that had to be enlarged to at least size eighteen, was a message that read: "Drop out of the race or I'll expose your record."

"I didn't send that, and I have no idea what record they're referring to."

The red of her face darkened another shade, from either embarrassment, anger, or both. "My juvenile record, you...you wicked witch."

Now, that hurt. I'd always pictured myself as

Glinda the Good Witch. "Those records are sealed. I don't have access to them."

She crossed her arms. "Well. my, my, aren't you the resourceful one."

"I didn't send it," I repeated. I was resourceful, but there was no reason for me to go searching for any dirt on Karen. She always managed to find trouble without my help.

"You couldn't stand the thought of me on the board, so you used the knowledge you gained to get me to drop out. Your name shows up as the sender of the message." She thrust the phone in my face again to make her point.

A thought occurred as my name in large font stared back at me. A thought besides the fact that Karen must have vision issues if she needed her display that large. "Why do you have me as a contact in your phone?"

"What?"

"For my name to show up, it means you have me saved as a contact in your phone. Otherwise, it would just show up as a number." I reached up and touched my name on her phone to open the contact. "That's not my number."

"Likely story," she scoffed.

"Dial it." I pulled my phone from my back pocket and unlocked it. I held it face up between us so she would see I wasn't hiding anything. "Dial the number."

She hit the number and initiated the connection. On her side, the phone rang and rang, but my phone stayed silent and provided no indication of an incoming call. I studied the number and committed it to memory, hoping I could use it to learn who actually did blackmail her and–I sighed inwardly–why.

After about six rings, she hung up. "That means nothing. You wouldn't be stupid enough to use your own phone."

"But I'd be stupid enough to make sure my name showed up? That doesn't make any sense, Karen." Never mind that I had no idea how to even make something like that happen. Maybe there was an app for that?

She tossed the phone on the counter. "None of this makes any sense. One night. One mistake. One moment in all the moments of my life that I regret more than anything else. I paid my debt to society. Why can't society forgive, forget, and let me live my life?"

Karen went behind the bar and my nerves went on high alert. Had I mentioned she and Richard owned guns? Instead of a weapon, she lifted a bottle of scotch and poured herself a generous glass. After a few swigs, she laughed. "You know what really ticks me off?"

Not wanting to take any chances there still might be a gun, I simply shook my head. Hey, if I had weapons hidden around my house, a liquor cabinet under a bar would be an ideal place (in addition to the bathroom).

"I wasn't the only one who did time because of that night. But did she get a threatening text the night of the election? No. No, she did not. How is that fair?"

Of the remaining women involved in the election, my brain quickly narrowed it down to two possibilities. It had to be Denise or Jackie. My money was on Jackie, given all I'd learned a short time ago. At least a few pieces of the puzzle might be falling into place. "It's not fair."

Sensing I had a limited time to say anything before she kicked me out, I needed to confirm my hunch. "Since those records are sealed, who else but the other person would know? Someone from their family?" I asked the question, reasonably assuming it had to be Lester. I just needed Karen to confirm.

She poured another measure of scotch, much smaller this time, and grabbed water from the mini fridge at the edge of the bar before sitting down on the couch opposite me. "Why would I tell you anything? I'm still not convinced you weren't the one behind this. I'm betting you weren't going to vote for me, anyway, so why not ensure no one else can?"

I didn't have time for this, so I offered her the same directness she'd always given me. "You're right, I wasn't. Tessa and Denise are getting votes from me. I'm still deciding on the last one." As I made my admission, I studied her closely to see if naming Denise got any reaction. My gut told me this was all tied to Jackie and Lester, but it was always best to be sure.

Her head lolled back against the soft cushions of the couch. "I get it. You and Tessa are friends. I'm not sure Denise is the right person for the job, though."

"And you think Jackie is? Truth be told, I'm not

entirely convinced about Denise, either. She certainly is passionate about whatever her current cause is. That can be an asset."

"Oh please, we both know the only thing she's passionate about is Alan Knightly. Like she has a chance with him."

She made a valid argument. "We may actually be in agreement about that point."

Karen lifted her glass. "Well, that's something to toast to."

Figuring I'd try to build on this moment, I lifted my glass and smiled. "Hear, hear." I also toasted myself for realizing I'd put a few things together. It was the first time today that had happened. This also led to the logical conclusion both Karen and Jackie had a juvenile record. And, it seemed, somehow Lester had been responsible for them getting caught. Thinking back to the fight between Jackie and Lester, the story almost made sense.

Almost.

Lester had to realize the information he used to destroy Karen's bid for election could also be used to destroy Jackie's chances as well. He'd made no secret, to Jackie at least, that he wasn't happy with her running. So, why not set me up to extort her rather than Karen? That part kept me solidly in the land of confusion.

After a few moments of silence, I noticed Richard peek his head around the corner. "Okay?"

Karen smiled. "We're fine, dear. Thanks for checking."

"Yup."

Another minute or so lapsed before she broke the silence. "If you're not here to further extort me, what do you want?"

Since we were on common ground, I didn't want to set her off again, but it was time to test additional theories and conclusions. "Is that why Richard beat Lester up? You guys figured it was him that supplied the information to whomever extorted you?"

She sat up straighter, and I could see a denial getting ready to form. Might as well stop that before it even started. "I just came from the marina. I overheard Jackie and Lester fighting. I know it was Richard. You're obviously irritated Jackie didn't get blackmailed. It had to be her or Lester that ratted you out. Brings me to only one conclusion: You and Richard figured it out and he went over to make Lester pay."

"You think you know everything, don't you?"

"Not really," I laughed. "If I did, I'd know why you threw your support to Jackie. I'd also know who really killed Miles and get them charged with the crime instead of me."

"That's right. Ms. High and Mighty has been arrested for murder. Which makes one wonder how you're out roaming the streets right now? I pull a prank that goes wrong and have to serve six months in a juvenile home, which, by the way, is only because that snake Lester ratted us out in the first place. However, you commit murder and you're free to walk around? Gotta love our justice system."

This was not headed in the direction I wanted. "First, I'm being accused of voluntary manslaughter, *not* murder. Second," I lifted my pant leg to display my newest accessory, "I'm not just free to roam around. And third, you still haven't explained why you put your support behind Jackie, after everything that transpired."

"Whatever. It's not like I care about you or what happens to you. As for your last statement, you're a smart girl. You'll figure it out."

Ouch, and here I thought we had a temporary truce. I also felt like she had more faith in me figuring things out right now than I had in myself. "I know you don't care about me, that's not a surprise. As for who you support, I probably will figure it out, but since I don't really care, I'll save the discovery for a day when I have nothing else going on. I do believe, however, Richard was the one who beat on Lester because he ratted you out again."

"That was part of it."

"And the other part?"

"Doesn't matter. Our agreement ends with Denise's main motivation."

"Try me. What won't we agree on now?"

She only hesitated a moment before answering. "You think Miles was bad news."

Not only did I *think* he was bad news, I knew it.

"What makes you think he wasn't? You couldn't have known him very long."

Karen shrugged. "Miles had a vision."

"And you wanted to be a part of it." I based this statement on the information Pete had provided.

"Is that so wrong?"

I sighed. "Not if his intentions were pure. I suspect that was only partially true."

With my admission, Karen sat up straight, her black shoulder length hair moving back and forth as she shook her head. She fastened her dark chocolate gaze directly on me. "Interesting how you pick and choose the people you see the good in. Ironic how we're never on the same page with that trait."

She garnered no immediate response from me. I was entirely too tired to argue tonight. When she said nothing further, I opted for a simple, "Perhaps, because we look at different things."

She relaxed back into the gray, overstuffed cushion. "Doesn't matter, anyway, He didn't want me to be a part of it."

"He turned down your money?" I'd not seen that coming, though I had suspected it as a possibility as I mulled over motives for murder.

"Yes."

"What about JB or Ted?"

Her eyebrow arched. "They were investing, too? Maybe Miles wanted it to be a good ol' boys club like everything else around here."

"I think they were interested, but I don't believe

they did. It's just a hunch based on observation. JB looked ill Monday night at the forum. You certainly weren't yourself. And, other than a brief glance, I didn't really pay attention to Ted, so he could be the anomaly here."

"And you think that is somehow connected to Miles' death?"

This time, I was the one who sank back in the cushions. "Honestly, I don't know. The only thing I'm certain of right now is two things. One, I didn't kill him. And two, I'm being framed."

Maybe it was the look of desperation on my face. Maybe Karen had a heart after all. Maybe it was for another reason entirely. But, whatever the reason, she stood up and moved over to sit next to me. Her voice was low as she admitted, "The other reason Richard beat Lester up was because Lester implied the time I spent with Miles was not merely for business reasons."

You have no idea how tempted I was to tease that maybe Lester was on to something, but deep down I didn't believe it for a moment. Also, it would destroy the temporary truce and information sharing happening. "I have no doubt he was wrong. No one who has ever been around you two would question that you love each other deeply and are obviously made for one another."

My words were not only true but hit the center target of the right thing to say. She smiled. "We are a match made in heaven."

"Agreed."

Her gaze turned intense again. "What I'm about to tell you is the last part of our peace pact."

"Understood." I wanted to ask why, but maybe a part of her really did feel sorry for me being falsely accused. Whatever the reason for her sharing, I would take it.

"As Richard was doing his number on Lester, he got him to share a piece of information that may be helpful."

"You have my undivided attention."

"Lester repeatedly denied he was the one who sent the text message. Richard told him he better come up with a convincing alternate theory." She smiled. "I love it when he gets all macho while still sounding brilliant."

Personally, I would have loved to hear how he did all of that with only one word, but that was beside the point. Instead, I smiled and nodded in encouragement for her to continue.

"Anyway, Lester admitted he shared the info with a woman at the bar Friday night."

"Why would Lester share a family secret with a random stranger?"

She arched her eyebrow, implying I'd asked the most ridiculous question ever. "Let's see...a below average man, a beautiful woman, and alcohol. Under those circumstances, a man would divulge where Hoffa's body was buried if he knew."

Karen was full of valid points tonight. Under the influence of alcohol, men could be convinced to share a lot of information, especially by a beautiful woman paying him extra attention. "Did Lester know who the woman was?"

She shook her head. "But he got a description. Thin, dark brown hair, and I quote, the most intense green eyes he'd ever seen."

A lump lodged in my throat. While that description could fit thousands, if not millions, it also fit one woman who was very much a person of interest in my current search for justice.

Natalie Dawson.

Chapter Eleven

I let her statement sink in for a moment before tucking it away for later. "Maybe we'll get lucky and find her so she can tell us if she was the one who blackmailed you. She also could have sold the information to someone else who had more of a vested interest in the outcome of the election. Maybe someone would pay for that kind of intel to use against you."

"I suppose, but I still think it's doubtful. Even if they did, why frame you? Why blackmail me, and not Jackie or both of us?" Karen appeared as perplexed as I was, especially by my last question.

I shrugged my shoulders. "I don't know." This was only a half truth. If it truly was Natalie who initiated the blackmail, I understood exactly why she picked me as the scapegoat. I didn't understand, however, why she would have only blackmailed Karen and not Jackie.

"We'll never know. I must accept that and move on."

"Sometimes, that's all we can do."

I let a few moments of silence pass between us before asking one more question that had been bouncing around in my brain at odd times over the past few days. "Why were you out wandering the streets early on Saturday morning?"

The question caught her attention, and her gaze narrowed. "What are you talking about?"

Either she didn't remember, or we were back to playing games. "Early Saturday morning, I'd just had a visit from Deputy Jake. He was leaving, and I saw you walking aimlessly down the sidewalk in front of my house. No disrespect, but I've never seen you out walking. You're always in your golf cart."

"Can't a girl go for a walk around here without someone questioning her motives?"

"Not around here. Anything outside the norm brings about questions."

She stood, and the expectant look she sent in my direction indicated I should follow her lead. I guessed I'd worn out my welcome. I rose from the couch and handed her my wine glass. Sadly, I'd only managed a couple of sips. Such a shame as it was a good vintage. However Karen and Richard had made their fortune, they'd done well.

"Thanks for stopping by." She set our glasses down on the bar.

I didn't move. Instead, I studied her face intently as I made my next statement. "Fine. If you won't tell me, I'll have to draw my own conclusions."

"Such as?" She crossed her arms, challenging me with her gaze.

"Such as you were out wandering the streets just an hour or so after Miles' estimated time of death. You were angry at Miles for not letting you invest. Maybe you decided if he didn't want your money, he wasn't going to get any. Or maybe Richard's jealous streak drove him to take matters into his own hands. Chief Parker indicated this was most likely a crime of passion based on the evidence. I could put this puzzle together easily based on circumstantial evidence. Which, I might add, is all they have on me."

If looks could kill, she wouldn't need to pull out a gun. Those dark eyes, now filled with rage, would be capable of dispersing shots equal to that of an AR15. Instead, she relied on verbal bullets. "Get out. Now."

And our temporary truce was over.

It had been a calculated risk putting it all out there, but at this point, I had to come up with alternate theories of the crime for my attorney. Might as well test them out before my trial. I didn't wait to be escorted to the door. Once outside, I exhaled slowly to release a little tension.

Did I really think she killed Miles? No. But something about the events of that night and into the morning weren't adding up. Behind the rage in her eyes, I'd seen something else. Fear, maybe? Was she afraid I'd figured out she was the killer? Or maybe my theory about Richard hit closer to home than she liked? I really needed to move the scale to find a balance between all the questions and answers. Right now, the questions were winning by a landslide.

On the way home, an idea occurred to me as to how to learn at least one answer. I pulled out my phone, entering the passcode before opening the app that would provide end-to-end encryption for a conversation. I dialed the number and felt a small sliver of warmth as the person on the other end answered. "Who would you like to speak to?"

"Virginia Oldoini, please?"

There was a long pause. This communication protocol was established by my team as a way to ask for help in a way that kept whoever might be listening in the dark about the true nature of the call. The names we chose helped identify the type of information needed. The team member who handled those phone calls, both now and then, was Jessica Villanova. She was an IT whiz kid whom I might have saved from doing time for hacking into various financial entities and creating general mayhem. As her way of saying thank you, she came to work for us and put her talents to use for good.

"Who's calling?"

Hearing her voice flooded my memories with the good ol' days. Even though the possibility anyone was still listening in was minimal, it warmed my heart that even though she knew it was me, she kept with the code we'd designed. "Luisa Zeni."

"Good to hear from you, Luisa. How can I help you today?" I could almost hear the smile in her voice.

Both Virginia and Luisa had been influential women in Italian history, part of the reason the duo had been chosen. While sometimes the names of the people used provided the code, in this case it was the next phrase that held the true reason for the call.

"I've lost ten of my sheep and don't know where to find them." This signaled that the information shared next would be a phone number I needed traced to obtain a location.

"Tell me more."

Now came the challenging part, weaving a story that made some sense and provided the numbers from the contact on Karen's phone. My gut told me the person who arranged the cloaked message was Nat. I needed to know where she was. "It started around two in the afternoon. Eight of the sheep were eating, but then when I counted again, one was missing, leaving only seven. I looked for four hours until around six. Then, I rested until about nine, but knew I had to get back at it since I'd found zero so far. Then, one came home with a friend, making my find a total of two."

"I'm glad you were able to locate almost all your sheep. I'll see what I can do to help you find the last one."

"Thank you." There was so much more I wanted to say, but doing so would bring another round of emotions I couldn't handle right now. Jessica and I had been very close. She'd always been like a younger sister. We bonded quickly and had spent many hours together planning jobs. Maybe when all of this was over, a family reunion of sorts would be in order. It would require careful planning and the utmost care, but getting to see them again would do my heart good. Of course, that was if Natalie and/or Dante weren't currently trying to frame me for murder. Otherwise, talk about an awkward family gathering.

"You're welcome. Watch your mailbox."

Knowing the results would be emailed to Luisa's account, there was nothing left to do but move forward. My gut also whispered that Dante had tried to tell me something in that holding room. But between the rumbling in my stomach and the fog settling in my brain from exhaustion, I couldn't process the meaning. Down deep, I couldn't accept he would outright betray me. A conversation with him, without Natalie around, would be the most helpful. This is why Jessica figuring out Nat's location was imperative. If they were together, it would be far more difficult. I held on to the belief they would follow the training we'd established for jobs. If they were, protocol dictated they would have separated by now to protect each other.

Once at home, I decided it was too early for bed, regardless of how tired my body and brain felt. I had no desire to cook, but the rumbling in my stomach sent a not-so-subtle warning. I needed sustenance. Because of my new ankle accessory, I couldn't venture too far away from home, certainly not far enough away that the potential for being recognized as a prime suspect in the latest headlines wouldn't happen. As a result, I decided to stay in town and face the proverbial public opinion music. It was going to happen sooner or later. I couldn't stay hidden away in my house and solve a murder.

I changed into dress pants. No sense in needlessly inviting scrutiny by exposing my legs and my new accessory. The black pants were paired with a red silk blouse. My hair was fashioned in a loose up-do with tendrils falling in soft waves around my neck and face. I chose black high heeled shoes. I might be hiding my ankles, but heels prompted me to walk with purpose. Never mind how uncomfortable my feet would be when I got home. I liked dressing up and looking my best, even if I felt anything but beautiful after the events of the day. The ensemble was finished with black onyx and silver jewelry, a gift from my parents when I graduated from college.

The trip to The Club was short, and the crowd was thin when I walked in. Official happy hour time slots didn't start until Wednesday. A quick check of my watch revealed it was around eight in the evening, most people had probably already eaten their dinner by now. This had to be the longest day ever.

"Would you like a table, ma'am?" The young lady working the hostess stand asked.

"Can I sit at the bar?' While I had no issue with eating alone, I'd learned people often felt sorry for people sitting at a table by themselves. For some reason, sitting at a bar by oneself led to less judgment. Weird how society interpreted essentially the same thing so differently.

"Of course."

I made my way across the large room, past the beautiful stone fireplace, to the bar, ignoring the looks and whispers I knew were taking place. Thankfully, at this time of night, it was probably folks who were lonely, extra social, or just didn't want to cook. I would only admit to one of those three.

Sitting at the corner of the bar was none other than James Cutter, looking like he'd lost his best friend. Or, more aptly, his business partner. I had no idea if he knew I'd been charged with Miles' death, but I figured there was no better time than the present to find out. "May I sit here?" I gestured to the empty bar stool next to him.

He stood quickly. "Of course, ma'am."

The smile on my face was genuine. I swear, no matter how bad a day could get, being on the receiving end of gentlemanly behavior added a little warmth to my spirit. "Thank you, sir."

James gestured to the bartender. "I'll have another and..." He looked to me. "Can I buy you a drink?"

How could a gal say no to such a generous offer? "Thank you. Pinot noir, please."

"Coming right up."

I turned to James. "Thank you, that was very kind." I noticed the amber liquid in his glass. "What are you having?"

"Maker's Mark, straight up. Been that kind of week."

And it was only Tuesday. Our drinks were delivered, and I lifted the wine glass toward him. "I hear that."

Though he smiled, it didn't reach his eyes. I still thought my week had to have been worse than his, but there was no sense in trying to one-up on that detail. After placing my food order, I turned toward James. "Regardless of how I felt about your business partner, I am sorry for your loss."

He sighed. "I appreciate that. After looking into him a bit more, there might have been some merit to your claims about his duplicitous intentions."

"Would you still have been his partner, after learning what you did?" I needed to know.

He turned and studied me intently with the darkest green eyes I'd ever seen. After a moment, he turned back to his drink. "I guess we'll never know."

I guess not. Time to shift gears a bit. "For what it's worth, it sounds like his public intention to help create plants that were drought resistant was a great idea. Is it really possible?"

My question brought a small sliver of light to his expression. "Oh yes, very possible. The science is convincing."

"Why not continue the work then? Your family certainly has more than enough money to fund such an endeavor. What an impact that could have, not only in Texas but in other drought-prone states or countries."

The momentary uptick of his demeanor soured, and the dark cloud returned. "Miles made sure I didn't know any of the other players, especially the scientists and genetic engineers with whom he'd worked on the concept. He said it was a need-to-know kind of thing."

My guess was because the brains behind this operation had nefarious intentions. I might not know exactly what his evil plans were, but I had no doubt vengeance on the company or people he felt betrayed him was at the top of his list. "I understand you'd have to start over, but given the potential impact, wouldn't it be worth the effort?"

He shook his head. "You wouldn't understand."

He was right. I didn't. However, it did appear he was done chatting about this. I'd add yet another mystery to the growing list of things to figure out. Admittedly, it wouldn't rank high on the list right now. I had plenty to ponder on in the future, though.

My pasta was delivered, the aroma of the spices and sauce renewed my desire and need for food. If that wasn't enough, the ferocious growling sound from my stomach sealed the deal. Since James wasn't interested in conversation anymore, I decided I would do my best to enjoy the meal.

Out of the corner of my eye, I continued to study him as I ate. He was on his third glass of the good stuff, or at least, the third one since I'd arrived. He made no effort to resume any kind of conversation, but there was one more piece of information I hoped he would share about. "Will you tell me a little bit about Cutter Cares?"

My question must have caught him a little off

guard. He turned his barstool to face me. "What do you mean?"

It wasn't a tough question. There was no secret his family operated under the umbrella of that company motto. But we'd both had a bad week, so I would clarify. "From what I understand, it's the guiding principle your family's company does all business by. How did that come about? What criteria do you use to determine what companies you invest in, et cetera?"

"With all due respect, ma'am, I don't think that's really any of your business."

I raised my hands in a surrendering gesture. "My apologies. I was just curious. It sounds like a wonderful way to do business in the world."

"Yeah, well, it's a lot more challenging to live up to that name and principle than you might think. Lots of strings attached to everything you want to do."

Whether he would believe me or not, I did understand that. All the good my team had done over the past decade or so had come at a cost. Right now, the personal price was very high for me. Despite it all, I still believed the good we'd accomplished made even what I was facing right now worth it. "Doing the right thing always challenges us. That's why it can often be very difficult. For what it's worth, I still believe it's the best way to go."

Believing our conversation was over, I signaled for my check. When the bartender brought it over, James moved his hand over and covered it. "I've got this."

"That's not necessary."

He offered me a slight smile. "It's the right thing to do."

Now, how could a girl turn that down after the speech I'd just given? I placed a hand on his shoulder. "Thank you for the dinner and drink. Don't give up on your dream. It's a wonderful one, and I have no doubt you can make it happen. If you decide to move forward, I'd be happy to invest in the project as well."

He cut me a quick look, unreadable yet intense. Maybe he did know I'd been charged and figured my money would do him no good once I was behind bars. Of course, it could just be the fact he didn't need my money or some other completely unrelated reason. Who knew? Not me. Instead of trying to get him to talk, I patted his arm and said, "Have a nice evening."

A nod was his only answer. Well, at least I tried. I started to step away, but I wanted to make one final attempt to ease his guilt. "Mr. Cutter?"

He looked up, and the despair in his gaze made me forget about my own troubles for a moment. I stepped closer. "Listen, I've seen a side of Miles you probably didn't have the benefit of knowing before you got into business with him. He was a con artist. I studied people like him in my psychology classes." This was better than admitting I'd also been a grifter (sounded better than a con artist) for the last ten or so years. The difference was that I conned the bad guys to get justice for the good ones. Miles had done the opposite.

Though he didn't say anything, he hadn't looked away, so I continued. "One of the seven basic ways someone cons another person is using the deception principle. They create a scenario, making you believe in whatever lie they're selling. They manipulate you and by the time you realize what's happening, it's too late. Your money, your confidence, or whatever it is they want from you, is being used for their benefit. Miles was gifted at deception. He got away with it in a large corporation for decades before he was caught. Don't beat yourself up too much for not seeing his ulterior motives."

"If you knew this, why didn't you say something when you learned he was in town? Why didn't you warn anyone? How was he not in jail if he did all the things you claim?" The tone of his voice rested somewhere between disbelief and disappointment.

"You have no reason to believe me, I know." The admission was made with a sigh. "But I didn't know he was in town until Friday afternoon. When I saw him with you that evening, I did try to warn you."

He laughed. "Acting like a jilted lover and hurling accusations in public aren't really the best ways to convince others your version of the truth is the right one."

Jilted lover? I replayed the conversation in my head. Maybe without context one could draw that conclusion, but my calling him by a different name should have alerted him there was something more to the story. Of course, Miles making his little comment about not knowing what my name was now (since I, of course, used an alias when running the con on him) probably threw some shade on my accusation.

The worst part of James' accusation, though, was the question about why he wasn't in jail. Nat had demanded the same answer. He had done jail time, just not much. All I could come up with was that, at the time, I'd felt we'd found justice for those he'd hurt. Maybe I naively believed after being publicly disgraced, he would turn from a life of crime and become a good citizen.

How wrong I'd been.

"I'm sorry my actions weren't enough to prevent you from being hurt by all of this. Truly, I am."

His gaze pierced mine for a moment longer before returning to his drink. "It doesn't matter, anyway, now. Time to figure out how to move on."

Thinking about how hard it had been for me to move on from the past, I couldn't provide much advice. I offered a sad smile, even though he was no longer looking at me. "I have no doubts you will."

There was no response, so I made my way out of the restaurant and down the steps. I'd parked in the back section of the lot, near some stately trees. When I unlocked the truck, the hair on the back of my neck stood straight, sending a chill scurrying down my spine. In the darkness, it would be impossible to see anyone, but I felt a presence. Casually, pretending to turn my neck to pop it and relieve some tension, I surveyed the inky black area. Nothing.

I waited a moment longer to see if anything

happened, but only silence and stillness met me. Great, now paranoia was setting in. Once the door was opened and the interior light kicked on, I did a visual survey inside with a quick glance to the bed of the truck to ensure no one was lying in wait. Still nothing.

Time to go home.

By the time I reached my garage, my internal warning system had calmed to a regular threat level status. Fear lingered on the outskirts of my mind. I'd learned to trust my gut and those feelings a long time ago. Maybe being out of the game had thrown it out of whack? Or maybe, I was just exhausted both mentally and physically. Either was a possibility. I headed inside, weary from the events and emotions of the day.

Too wound up to sleep just yet, I pulled out the laptop to update my notes. I reviewed the list:

Miles changed his last name and convinced James Cutter to invest in a new business.

James made an initial investment. Possibly other investors as well. Potential that one of the investors (most likely James?) was going to invest more in a little over 30 days. No idea why.

Time of death estimated between 4 and 5 a.m. Saturday morning.

Miles likely knew his attacker.

Dante left my home sometime in the middle of the night.

Odd piece of yellow plastic found in the wooded area where the murder occurred.

Natalie had made it her mission to make Miles' life difficult.

Dante brought in for questioning.

Dante tells me to be smart and to remember Zig Zag job.

Before I spent too much time analyzing what I'd already written, I added:

Pete shares that Karen, JB, and Ted were additional potential investors besides James Cutter.

Odd behavior at the forum: Karen withdraws, JB looks ill.

I'm arrested. My knife is found somewhere near the crime scene.

Charged with voluntary manslaughter, not murder. Kelsey posts my bail.

EZ reveals Richard's hands had blood on them the morning of Miles' death. He and Karen were fighting.

Richard beat up Lester for sharing Karen's juvie record, possibly with Nat.

Jackie Price's juvie record remains a secret.

James says he can't continue the project, and that I wouldn't understand why.

Deciding sometimes looking at paper rather than a screen helped, I printed my notes. Thankfully, I'd not done this before. The police would've loved finding this. They probably would have laughed at the details I'd thought were important. The knife line might have captured their attention. Armed with a Texas gold bar and glass of water, I moved to my back deck. After a few deep breaths, I reviewed the list again. Miles was a skilled con artist who understood there were thousands of variations on seven basic ways to "persuade" people to do what you wanted.

There was no doubt James had been subjected to a combination of two principles: deception and need/greed cons. Miles' game plan must have involved playing to what he learned James wanted most out of life and then capitalizing on that to make him susceptible to being deceived. Other than a potentially solid investment, what was in it for James? His family already had more than enough money to last them for generations. There had to be something more for Miles to manipulate him so successfully.

I had no doubt a time principle con was being used on me. Someone had skillfully guided me into a situation where time was limited and the stakes were high. This prompted people to act out of character and not follow the same guidelines or strategy they normally employed.

Was that happening here? By framing me for murder (or manslaughter), was someone trying to make me approach things in a different way than I had in the past? More importantly, was Natalie or Dante doing that to me? Sadly, they were the most logical conclusions given everything that had happened. What path were they trying to lead me down? If anyone knew how I thought and approached challenges, it would be someone from my team. They'd watched how my mind worked for over a decade.

My eyes closed with the hurtful realization they

could be behind all of this. Natalie must truly hate me for not putting Miles away when we had the chance. While throwing a pity party for myself never lasted long, I did allow myself about ten minutes to sulk.

The full moon reflecting off the glassy water of Lake Amore mirrored the light shining down, filling the night with such beauty. Despite all the trouble, I still loved everything about this town. Okay, maybe a couple of the people I didn't love so much, but there's always a little bit of bad with the good, right?

Moving inside, I grabbed my laptop. It was reasonable to assume Miles had to obtain permits to build the lab to carry out vengeance on his prior employer. As permits such as those were part of the public record, I surfed the Internet until I found the Crockett County website where one could search and learn things. I typed in Miles Grant's name and hit enter. Thanks to the miracles of modern technology, an entry appeared on the screen.

Noting the location on my paper, I opened Google maps and entered the address. I zoomed in to learn more about the surrounding area. My heart dropped a bit when I realized it was five to ten minutes, depending on traffic, outside the county line. This meant I would have a maximum of twenty minutes, possibly less, once I reached the facility to get in, see if there was anything there that might help me learn who had motive to kill Miles, and then get back across the county line before my ankle bracelet signaled my transgression to all surrounding law enforcement. That scenario needed to be avoided. My mind briefly pictured the disappointment on Kelsey's face should this occur. She wouldn't be happy, and let's be real, neither would I.

It was a risk. A big risk, but it needed to be done. My preliminary hearing was scheduled for Friday morning. That left two days to find the real killer and prove my innocence. Not a lot of time, but if I couldn't do it in that timeframe, there was a good chance I would never be able to.

Before I shut the laptop down, I pulled up Facebook to see if there'd been any more posts about the candidates. Voting started at midnight, I believed, so there had probably been a few posts to catch up on. I'll admit, I was also checking to make sure my name or mug shot hadn't been plastered all over social media. On the community Facebook page, there was a pinned post outlining an apology to Alan Knightly for falsely misrepresenting his voting record to the community. It was an anonymous post, but it was safe to assume whoever the woman had been who spread those rumors in the first place was no longer serving as part of the editorial community here in Wilson.

I scrolled down a little more and saw a post by Karen Bizzy. She was sharing her full support for Jackie. Closing my eyes, I tried to put myself in Karen's shoes. Karen and Jackie must have been friends as teenagers. They got into trouble when a prank went wrong. Both spent time in juvie as a result. Only Karen was blackmailed. Why would she support Jackie?

After a few moments of contemplative silence, I heard a chorus of angels belting the Hallelujah chorus. It made perfect sense now. Just as someone blackmailed Karen to secure her cooperation, she could use the same threat against Jackie to ensure she supported Karen's agenda. Since they shared the same secret, it came down to mutually assured destruction.

Weariness seeped into my bones. It was time for bed, even if the clock only read a little after nine. Tomorrow was a new day. And tomorrow, I vowed to make progress and start to tie up all these loose ends. I sent a quick prayer to the heavens that all the tying wouldn't create a rope long enough on which my enemies could hang me.

Chapter Twelve

Sleep was for the weak. At least, that's what I told myself when five in the morning rolled around. While normally a morning person, my dreams–or nightmares, depending on how you chose to look at them–were filled with random images. Karen waving a gun at me right before I saw Emerson running away from the woods heading toward me in a zig zag motion. Before I could jump out of the way, Natalie appeared and attacked me. Her sticky ring pop getting tangled in my hair. The entire time, Dante watched and just kept shaking his head as a parent might show their disappointment in an errant child.

It was better to just get up, hit the shower, and get ready for the day. I dressed in fleece-lined black pants, a black long-sleeved shirt, and finished the ensemble with a black sweater. My hair was pulled back into a messy bun. No one needed their hair getting in the way when they were trying to break into a building.

Thankfully, there wasn't much traffic before six. I checked my speed (no use drawing unnecessary attention to myself) and made my way to the county line in about fifteen minutes. I stopped just before the boundary and pulled over to the side of the road. I studied the online map and layered the view to show satellite pictures from when the map was created. It might not be one hundred percent accurate, but it would give me an idea of the layout. If all went according to plan, this would help me get in and out as quickly as possible.

Now that the mental and logistical preparations were complete, the only thing left to do was set a silent timer on my watch for twenty-five minutes and allow myself a couple of deep breaths to release a small measure of the death grip that tension had on my nervous system. Knowing this was as good as it was going to get, I put the truck in drive and started the timer. The area where the address was located was in a warehouse district. The landscape was dark and foreboding at this time of morning. The dusk to dawn lights were on, but the fog-covered ground was reminiscent of the start of one of those B-reel horror flicks my sister liked to watch.

Ignoring the heebie-jeebies, I parked in the corner of the lot, moving quickly and quietly to the building denoted on the permit. Construction appeared to be still underway, but I could hear noise coming from inside. Who in the world, besides me, would be here at this time of morning? The windows were covered with blackout paper, which indicated–to me, at least–that whatever was going on in that part of the building must have been the evil part of Miles' plan. I tested the knob of one of the doors farthest away from where the sound originated. Of course, it was locked. My handy-dandy lock picking set was called into use once again. The ability to get into places I didn't have a key for had served me well over the years.

Wiping the dampness from my hands, the lock became my sole focus. Carefully moving the interior pieces around until the telltale click was heard, I gave myself a high five that this skill remained intact. The flashlight app on my phone was called into service. Using the dimmest setting, it allowed me to see without being seen.

After a short walk down the hall, peering into rooms with unlocked doors, I managed to locate Miles' office. There was no personalization to give it away, but I'd been in his evil lair the last time he'd spun his web of deceit. The lone photo of Niccolo Machiavelli gave it away. Miles believed in the Machiavellian principle: Immoral acts were justified if they helped one achieve political glory. While I didn't believe for one moment Miles had political aspirations, he sought glory and, most importantly, financial gain. He certainly hadn't cared who he'd hurt in the process.

I could reminisce about Miles and all the wrong turns he'd taken in life another time. Now, I needed to see if there were any clues about his killer just laying around. A quick visual survey revealed no papers or other blue light specials for motive sitting on the desk or bare shelves. A file cabinet stood proudly in the corner, taunting me with its potential secrets.

The top drawer was tested. Locked, of course. He had been a careful mad man, right up to the point he pushed someone a little too hard and they pushed back. Retrieving my lock picking set again, I focused my attention on the mechanism for the file cabinet. I was about three seconds away from success when I heard footsteps and voices coming down the hall.

Adrenaline surged through my veins, prompting beads of perspiration to surface. I needed a place to hide, and I needed it now! The sparse furnishings didn't provide many potential safe havens. A quick visual survey revealed another door. I race-walked across the room, all the while praying the door wouldn't be locked. I also added a footnote to the request that it didn't open to a room full of bad guys.

For the first time in days, a small bit of luck favored me as the doorknob turned easily. I stepped inside and closed the door just before the footsteps and voices arrived. My flashlight provided enough illumination for me to determine my hiding place was a supply closet. From the looks of the sparse contents in the room, there was nothing hidden here that would give up any secrets. I confess to experiencing mild disappointment. In the crime shows on television, the good guys always seemed to stumble on some great clue while hiding from the bad guys. Oh well, this was real life, and the other was fiction. With no clues to keep me occupied, I pressed my ear to the door and listened.

The rapid beating of my heart paused as one of the voices registered as my once good friend and teammate, Natalie Dawson. What in the good Lord's name was she doing here so early in the morning besides talking to what had to be a bad guy or girl? Or, maybe this person had been manipulated by Miles as well.

"So, we're in agreement?" Natalie asked whoever was there with her.

"For that kind of money, I'll do whatever you want, lady."

"Good, let's work out the details. This needs to look like an accident."

My hand immediately covered my mouth to stifle the sound of surprise as I heard Natalie lay out her plan to the mystery man for destroying the building and, along with it, all the evidence inside. Ironically, she asked him to destroy the good along with the bad. The scientist was arguing with her about destroying both samples. He claimed their research demonstrated they were very close to being able to genetically modify the seeds and their subsequent plants to be drought resistant under even the most extreme of circum-stances. The sample 'B' research, he had admitted, gave him pause. From what I could understand, those genetic engineers had been tasked with creating the illusion of being the same as sample 'A.' However, when this particular seed was combined with typical pesticides, it would ultimately kill the crops.

If you were a criminal mastermind hell bent on revenge, it was a brilliant plan. Evil in its design, and devastating in the effects had they been allowed the time to continue their research until successful. I could see Miles's plan unfold in my head like a train wreck you couldn't look away from. He would set up his former enemies by showing them the good seed from the first sample. Once they saw the results, they would buy it in mass quantities to help them be proactive against the dry conditions they often faced. Miles would sell them, however, the seed with nefarious intent. Ultimately, the entire harvest would be killed before they would realize what happened.

One major crop fail would not only be devastating to an agriculture company and their farms for one season, but the damage to their reputation could bring about their ruin. Additionally, crop failure from a major supplier would have a tremendous impact on food supply. Large agriculture companies would sell to their customers in high volumes, who then would use the products to create the everyday things we know and love.

Miles would use the old bait and switch technique to bring his former employer to ruin. While the first seed would help many other companies and farmers, anyone Miles wanted revenge on would fall prey to his deception when he switched Seed A for Seed B.

Then, the thought struck me.

The Zig Zag job was originally named the Zing Zhang job after Zhang Yingu. He wrote *The Book of*

Swindles back in the early sixteen hundreds. Much of his book was devoted to variations of the bait and switch. Because Dante could never say Zing Zhang with a straight face, we renamed the op zig zag.

This is what Miles had done on multiple fronts. His ultimate goal was to convince his enemies of the merit of his product based on one version of events. He then used the power of that possibility to entice them to buy the seeds in large quantities. Then, he would switch the good seed for the bad. By the time they realized it, the crops would be decimated.

Miles had been an expert at bait and switch scenarios. He used it on his former employer and obviously planned to use it again, this time hiding behind James as the face of the operation. The question remained why Dante wanted me to remember it. Had he already known this was Miles' plan? If so, why not share it with me from the beginning? We could have used that knowledge to give James proof, along with the local police.

The scenario didn't seem likely. Dante wanted Miles to pay for his actions as much as Nat did. If he had the knowledge to destroy him, he would've done so.

This left the question, who was doing the bait and switch Dante was warning me about? My watch buzzed quietly against my wrist. Only seven minutes to go before I needed to be across the county line and back to the safety of my court-ordered parameters. Natalie and this mystery man needed to hurry it up.

"Listen, I'm sorry. This is non-negotiable. If you want the money, then it all has to go. Understood?"

There was an audible exhalation of breath. "Understood."

"Tomorrow, just after midnight. Agreed?"

"Agreed."

With the timing for the destruction of the evidence agreed upon, I finally heard footsteps retreat from the office. I checked the countdown clock on my watch. Five minutes and thirty seconds. I couldn't delay leaving any longer. If I stayed, I risked not making it back in time, which I expected would result in the county sheriff's office descending on my position. Part of me was tempted to let that happen to bring attention to this place and save it. However, determining the actual killer needed to take place first. I also wondered why Natalie didn't just destroy the building herself. Why hire someone else to do it? Any action at this point resulting in my return to jail would prevent me from having the freedom to find those answers. Natalie wanting to destroy his research didn't necessarily translate to her being a killer.

I was *still* missing something.

Unable to delay any longer, I quietly opened the closet door and peeked out. The office was empty. I pulled the lucky handkerchief that had been my grandfather's out of my back pocket and quickly wiped down any surface I had touched. If the police did show up here before the place was destroyed, there was no need for them to find my fingerprints at the scene. That wouldn't help prove my innocence.

Once the housekeeping details were complete, less than five minutes remained. Checking the hallway outside the office to ensure the coast was clear, I ignored the hammering of my heart as I headed for the exit. The temptation to run was strong, but my motto of never running taunted me from the back of my brain in time with the buzzing on my wrist. Maybe this was one time I should make an exception to that golden rule.

With my truck in sight, the constant buzzing on my wrist urged me to increase my pace. I might not have been running, but if racewalkers could see me now, they'd welcome a new champ onto their team. As I neared my method of escape, my sweaty palms dug into my pocket to unlock and remote start the truck. A small part of me was thankful I'd spent the extra money on this perk as it was certainly coming in handy.

Without even bothering with the seatbelt, I accelerated out of the parking lot, through the industrial park, and onto the highway without slowing down. Once on blacktop, I prayed no police officers were out this morning looking to add to their quota of speeding tickets for the month. The gas pedal met the metal of the floorboard while my focus remained on staying between the yellow lines. The beautiful rolling hills of ranches and stately trees appeared like a movie on fast forward just outside my window.

The buzzing stopped just before I crossed the county line. Had I made it in time? Had an alert already been sent out to everyone in the vicinity to apprehend the fleeing suspect? Now back in "safe" territory, I slowed to a normal speed. If they were going to come get me now, there was no sense in trying to outrun them. The GPS tracker in my ankle bracelet would make that a moot point.

My heart rate finally leveled out as I neared the stoplight where a left turn would take me down the long, winding road ending at the entrance to Wilson. But instead of getting in the turning lane, I decided to go straight. I needed to know whether I'd set off any alarms with my early morning antics. It was important to stay out of jail long enough to get answers to all the questions burning a hole in my brain. This meant I needed to go straight to the source. Better to be proactive with the opportunity to argue my case instead of law enforcement showing up at my door to arrest me... again. My neighbors deserved better.

The drive to the government complex in Crockett County took about thirty minutes. However, given how early it still was in the morning, I stopped at a little drive-through coffee shop and ordered a cappuccino and chocolate pastry. Hey, it could be my last meal outside of prison. It was important to choose wisely. Carbs, caffeine, and sugar always counted as great comfort food choices.

As I sat in the parking lot of the little café, I concluded that a conversation with Dante, and without

Natalie, needed to occur. For him to talk to me in code like that, he had to be trying to give me information without feeling like he was betraying his friendship with Natalie.

Before the team parted ways, we'd created a private group on a messaging board that only the four of us had access to. If anyone needed to communicate in an emergency, they would leave a coded message for the others to see. The problem I faced was being able to get a message out there that only Dante would understand.

Bringing the app out of deep sleep on my phone, I sipped my beverage and contemplated the best way to send the message. It took me until I finished the pastry and the tasty liquid caffeine to arrive at a possibility. Forcing my fingers not to tremble, I typed in the following message:

It's been a while since I've been fishing. The bait I have right now isn't working, time to switch it up. Then, at the perfect time, I will be successful surrounded by all that I love.

This post might lead my team to worry I'd lost my mind or forgotten the original purpose of this board. I couldn't be concerned with that detail, only that Dante would realize I understood his message (at least, in part) and wanted him to meet me at sunset on my back deck. Dante was smarter than he let on to the outside world. He loved to fish and had taught me the best time to try my luck at the sport was at sunset. Referencing all that I love hopefully indicated my house just as the sun began its disappearance for the evening.

With that detail accomplished, along with a sense of relief the police hadn't shown up to box me in at the coffee shop, I rewarded myself with another cappuccino and headed toward the sheriff's office. All right, that wasn't entirely honest. The game warden's office happened to be in the same complex. Jeremy's shift would be ending soon. Normally, he worked the mid-shift. However, I remembered a buddy of his was getting married, so he'd agreed to take the night shift for a few days to allow him some time with his new bride.

Since we'd been on the outs the past several days, I wanted to at least try to set things right before whatever happened in the next day or so made it much harder to mend the fence of our relationship. I now accepted we were too far apart to have anything more than a casual friendship, but I still wanted him in my life. Additionally, his buddies at the Sheriff's department knew he and I were somewhat close and, to date, they'd kept him abreast of all the items in my life that came across their desks. If I'd violated parole, I had no doubt they'd already reached out to share the news. Besides, it might be nice to go fishing for information with my favorite game warden. The thought made me smile, which was a welcome change from the reactions all my other thoughts this morning had brought about.

I stood next to his truck and waited. Thankfully, it didn't take long before he came out of the building.

The five o'clock stubble shadowed his chiseled jaw and only added to his rugged handsomeness. Watching him stretch and inhale the fresh morning air drew my attention away from his face and to the strength of his body. He took good care of himself, no one could deny that. I shook my head slightly to disburse the images and feelings for what could never be back into the recesses of my brain. Wanting to test the waters, I offered a small smile. "Good morning, Jeremy."

"Sadie? What are you doing here?"

"I wanted to see you."

The golden flecks in his hazel eyes flashed with confusion. "Is everything okay?"

The small chuckle escaped before I could stop it. "Honestly? Nothing is okay right now. I'm hoping things aren't worse now than they were when I woke up this morning."

"You're not making any sense." he sighed. "My brain is tired after being up all night, sorry."

I shrugged my shoulders. "Not even eight hours of restful sleep would allow my life to make sense. Although, it might be nice to give that a try."

His fingers brushed my cheek. "Tell me what's going on. Being arrested for manslaughter is a leap, even for you."

Tears threatened at the tenderness in his voice. Despite our disagreements and views on life, at his core, he was a sweet man who cared deeply for those around him. I stilled his hand against my cheek, savoring the warmth for a minute before releasing him and stepping back. I needed distance to say and do the things that must be done. "Before I answer you the best way I can, will you tell me if your buddies in the sheriff's department are going to be looking for me in the next few minutes?" I had no idea how long it took a violation of the county line to get reported and a team to be mobilized.

"Why would you think I would know? I've been out on patrol."

"Because the radio you wear during each shift keeps you connected and allows any news they might believe would be of interest to you to be shared." I lifted my hand to stop the protest forming on his beautiful lips. "You and I both know they tell you anything they learn about me."

The slight hint of red coloring his cheeks only added to his charm. "Okay, you have a point. But I promise you, there's been radio silence this morning where you're concerned."

A breath of relief escaped my lungs. Maybe there were a few seconds or minutes of grace period before an alarm went off. Good to know. Though exact knowledge of that timeframe would be useful information, I knew it was a moot point to ask Jeremy. Even if he knew, he wouldn't share for fear I'd take advantage of it. He would be right.

"I'm asking again. What's going on? I know we're not on the best of terms right now. I'm not sure we're ever going to be able to bridge the distance between us, but that doesn't change the fact I care about you. I don't want anything bad to happen to you."

Lack of sleep affected my ability to control my emotions, but I refused to cry in front of him. I was a strong, independent woman and that simply was not in my code of behavior. Instead, I nodded. "I understand. I can't change who I am or, more importantly, who I was no more than you can. For what it's worth, I didn't kill anyone. Never have."

"Sadie..." he started, but my hand went up to silence him.

"My past is catching up to me, though. My only regret, and I do mean only, is that the choices I made then are making it difficult for me to have a future now. We are too far apart to be anything more than friends, and maybe not even that. You see the world in black and white, good and bad. The lines are more blurred for me. You have absolute faith in the justice system. I've seen it fail good people time and time again. And while there are some lines I would never cross, I'm an 'ends justify the means' kinda gal. I know you do not subscribe to that philosophy."

He looked like he was going to say something, so I quickly moved forward. "And that's okay. It takes all kinds of people to make the world go round. You and I just aren't close enough in that circle of life to have a meaningful connection outside of what we've already shared. I wouldn't change you for the world, even if I might like to be able to change myself so we could have a future."

This time, he moved quickly and pulled me in for a hug before I could evade him. "Sadie, you are so hard on yourself. Please just tell me what's going on and let me help you. Whether we have any kind of future or not, it's too soon to tell. Even if we don't, I want to keep anything bad from happening to you."

After a couple inhales and exhales which allowed me to soak up that woodsy smell he always had no matter if it was the beginning or end of his shift, I stepped back and gave him a small smile. "I know, and that means a lot. But you can't help me this time. Tomorrow night, I'm going to try and fix a serious wrong my past choices have caused. If all goes well, maybe we can continue this conversation. But until I can effectively handle the fallout from my past, I can no longer give thought to the future. I'm sorry."

Before he could say anything else, I turned and moved quickly to my truck. I'd learned what I came to learn and said what I needed to say. There was nothing more to be accomplished here. I had a very small window of time to formulate my plan and try to do all the things that needed to be done.

Later, I would allow myself to mourn the loss of what could have been between the two of us. For now, my focus was on making sure I had some kind of future, whether it included Jeremy or not. Most importantly, I needed to make sure the future didn't include me spending the greater part of the rest of my life in a ten-by-ten windowless cell.

Chapter Thirteen

On the drive home, I started working through the various scenarios and timing to come up with the perfect plan. I did allow myself a small bit of joy remembering how we, like many others, would name our plans using letters of the alphabet, with Plan A being the most desirable outcome for each of the steps in our carefully constructed outline. Then, we moved our way through the alphabet as contingency plans were drawn up. Sometimes, for fun, we would each wager money or items we'd secured from previous jobs on which plan we thought we'd end on. For the official record, Plan A never won a bet. Usually, we landed somewhere around Plan E unless everything went wrong, then all bets were off. At that point, getting out of a situation with our lives and our freedom was all that really mattered.

I arrived home around ten in the morning. The temptation to stop in at Tesoro was great, but rest was needed more than the solace I found surrounded by the beauty of the creations in my shop. Exhaustion had been threatening for days now. I needed to give my body and brain a chance to recover before trying to put all the pieces together. Before I could close the garage door, I heard my name being called.

"Ms. Sadie!"

Emerson's voice cut through my jumbled thoughts, bringing a smile to my face. I joined him on the driveway. "Hey, nice scooter. You must have done the things your auntie wanted so you could get it."

A blush crept up his face. "Well, sort of."

You had to love teenage answers. "What does that mean?"

"She felt bad about me finding the body while I was trying to do something good for my community, so she kept me out of school yesterday as I had another interview with Chief Parker. After that, she took me to get the scooter."

I probably would have done the same thing. "That was very nice of her. I still think it's a good idea for you to try to complete the initial assignment."

"Yeah. Even though I really wanted the scooter, I felt bad about taking it, especially after talking to Mr. Cutter."

This was an interesting development. "When did you speak with him?"

"Yesterday afternoon. I delivered some flowers to the Cutter family home after school." He smiled. "He really liked my scooter." Then, I noticed his face fell somewhat.

"Why does that make you sad?" I was also curious who ordered flowers and why, but that was more being nosy than anything relevant to the matters at hand.

"I don't want to talk about it."

Color me surprised that a young man didn't want to talk about his feelings. Of course, neither did grown men, so there's that. "I think maybe you do. Otherwise, you wouldn't have brought it up."

He cut me a look but didn't offer any snark. His auntie really was raising him well. I waited while he appeared to be having an internal debate. I could only assume it was to decide if he would confide in me or jump on his scooter and ride away.

After a few tense moments, he let out a big sigh. "He asked me how I earned the money for the scooter."

While I thought it an odd question to ask a teenager, maybe he had a reason. "What did you tell him?"

"I told him the truth."

"You told him you found the body and your aunt felt bad so she bought it for you?"

The look he sent my way left no doubt I'd guessed wrong. Way wrong. "Of course not! I've only talked about finding the body with you, my auntie, and the police."

I know it's weird, but I felt honored I was included with those he felt comfortable (or compelled) to share that information with. "Okay, sorry. I'm just out here on a fishing expedition."

He cracked a small smile at my analogy. "I know, sorry. I'm still not good with talking about that."

"Understood. So, what did you share with him?"

"I told him my aunt had given me a way to earn the money. I figured he'd be happy about that."

"He wasn't?"

"Not really. He told me relying on other people to decide what I can and can't do isn't a good thing. If I wanted something, I needed to go out and make it happen and not let anything or anyone stand in my way."

Coming from the man who had appeared defeated a couple days ago while he drowned his sorrows in Maker's Mark made the advice a bit ironic. "There is some truth to what he's saying, but there should be limits on what people do to get the things they want. Something illegal or immoral isn't justified merely because you wanted something. And," I added out of respect for his aunt, "I think your auntie was just trying to teach you it's important to work for the things you want, not stand in your way."

Emerson nodded. "I know. I didn't think it was a bright idea to disagree with him, though. I wanted a good tip." He shared with a grin.

I laughed. "Nothing wrong with that. And because I know you, I'm betting you're still going to work on finding ways to help your community, aren't you?"

He grinned. "Yeah, I don't mind helping people. I just need to figure out how."

I gave him a quick hug. "I have no doubts you will do just that."

The shade of red on his face deepened. "Yeah, that's the plan. Anyway, the real reason I'm here is I wanted to tell you something."

"What's that?"

He stepped away and walked quickly to the steps leading up to my front door. He plopped down. Since I had no idea what was going on, I followed, taking a seat next to him. "You can tell me, whatever it is."

"I saw something else that morning."

He didn't need to elaborate which morning he was alluding to. It was the only morning in recent time that mattered, at least to me and Emerson. "Go on." I kept my tone level and calm, not wanting to alarm him in any way or stop the flow of information.

Emerson looked out into the distance. "Mr. Bizzy was there."

"At the crime scene?"

"Not exactly."

This might have been how Chief Parker felt when he was trying to get information out of me. If so, I owed him an apology. Exhaling slowly, I forced a smile. "Exactly where, then?"

"A couple blocks away. I'd just seen—"

"Mr. Gentry?" I figured there was no sense in referring to him merely as a dead body.

He nodded. "Mr. Bizzy seemed upset, and like he was looking for something."

"Or someone?" I supplied.

At my question, Emerson's gaze snapped to mine. There was a moment's hesitation before he answered, "Yeah, maybe."

"Maybe his wife? I saw her out walking that morning, too."

"Over by the condos?"

I shook my head. "No, on my street, but given the time I saw her and the time you saw him, it's possible she had been there earlier."

He closed his eyes, and a look of concentration settled over his features. The gears in his head had to be grinding. After a few minutes, his gaze found mine. "So, she could have been there when he was killed?"

This really wasn't a conversation I should have been having with a teenager, but given all that he'd witnessed I felt like he at least deserved an honest answer. "It's possible, but just because someone was in the area, doesn't make them the killer." I bumped his shoulder with mine. "I mean, you were kinda there, too, right?"

His smile told me I'd found the right words. "Yeah, I see what you're saying." He paused for a moment. "But it is still a possibility."

"Yes, she would have had an opportunity, but you know that's not all that's required."

"Right. Motive and means are in there, too."

"Exactly, and I don't think we even know the official cause of death yet." That detail had been bothering me. I mean, it was logical to assume if one found a bloody knife and there were knife wounds in the victim that it played a part, but something wasn't adding up. If it were that simple, Chief Parker would have just said, right?

"I'll see what I can find out," Emerson offered.

"Absolutely not. You've already been too close to this as it is. We must let the justice system do its thing, and you need to enjoy your new scooter."

Emerson stood. "Right, 'cause that's what you always do."

I could feign innocence, but Emerson had seen me in action before. He wouldn't buy it. "Fair enough, but I'm asking you to please stay away from this."

He leaned over and gave me a hug. "You worry too much, Ms. Sadie. I'll be all right."

I watched him ride away and sent up a quick prayer that he would stay safe. Once he was out of sight, I closed the garage and went inside for some much needed rest.

The nap did me some good. My thoughts were less jumbled, even if no answers had arrived in my sleep. One thing that had been made clear was the need to get to the bottom of whatever was bothering Kelsey. She had been nothing but a wonderful friend to me, and I owed her some time to make sure I could be there for her. A check of my watch showed it was half past noon. As I recalled, she met with other women downstairs at The Club to play bridge. Or maybe it was mahjong. Either way, she would be there.

The wardrobe choice was easy. Slacks, silk blouse, and wedge heels. My hair got swept back in an easy up-do (mostly to keep it out of my eyes) and my makeup was light. I wasn't trying to impress anyone, but it was important to at least be presentable. One never knew who they might meet while out and about.

Waiting until I knew everyone was downstairs, I quietly slipped through the foyer and made my way down the steps. There was a long hall that housed the offices for the staff. Thankfully, no one was hanging out there. Perhaps, they were at lunch or hobnobbing with the Wilson elite. Either way, I was grateful my presence was still unknown. In addition to a room used for bridal parties that boasted a wall-to-wall, floor-length mirror as well as multiple lighted make-up stations, there was another large area on the lower floor that included a fully stocked bar for guests to conduct business or host parties. Partitions were sometimes used to make the space into two separate meeting/party places. I hoped this was the configuration of the room today as it would be the only way I could listen in without being detected.

A quick peek around the corner proved that things were as I needed them to be. Quietly, I slipped into the adjacent room and positioned myself close to the movable wall to listen in. My plan was to learn whatever I could and then slip out to wait for Kelsey so we could speak in private. After a couple of deep breaths, I closed my eyes and listened.

"I'm so relieved they finally arrested that woman for poor Mr. Gentry's murder."

It didn't take a skilled investigator to realize I was *that* woman. The voice of the person bringing up this scintillating piece of gossip was none other than Dora Lee Birmingham. She was the Queen of the Elite here in Wilson.

"You can't seriously think she killed him, can you?"

My ongoing support system, Kelsey, defended me once again. This created a surge of warmth throughout my heart.

"They don't typically arrest someone without having proof, dear."

"Circumstantial proof."

A harumph followed a sigh from Dora Lee (at least, it was reasonable of me to assume it was her). "I'm sure both you and your husband are disappointed with the development. Although, it's understandable. I guess it didn't matter, from your perspective, if he was alive or dead. You had a lot to lose. Or perhaps it is lost already?"

This was news. I could see how Pete stood to gain internally in the law firm with Miles' business, but other than the added prestige and bonus, was there something else Kelsey hadn't told me? She'd been acting weird since we first started talking about the whole Miles situation and potential business deal.

"Can we please move on to other topics?" Kelsey's voice sounded strained.

"Of course, dear. I was just feeling troubled for you and wanted you to know I understand how disappointed you must be. Between your husband losing the deal, you losing a potential investment opportunity, and your friend betraying you, it's a lot to take in."

"I appreciate your concern, but let's not discuss my problems. They'll be there waiting for me once our card game has ended."

This information swirled around in my already crowded brain. Was Kelsey planning on investing with Miles and his venture as well? I recalled her sharing about Miles' vision and that drought resistant crops could be a game changer for not only Texas, but also many historically dry states. Honestly, it was the last part that bothered me most. Why did people believe I betrayed her? More importantly, did *she* believe it?

I'd heard enough. At least, now I had a reasonable theory on why Kelsey felt guilty. She'd withheld the truth from me about being an investor in Miles' business. She'd let Pete serve up Karen, JB, and Ted, but had kept their investment intentions a secret. Maybe once she'd heard the gossip about my encounter with Miles, she decided it was better not to tell me? And the alleged betrayal. I knew there were things I kept from her about my past, but I didn't view it as a betrayal. I kept my secrets to protect those I cared about. I needed to ask Kelsey about all of this. In my heart, I didn't believe she felt that way. We simply needed to clear the air.

My phone buzzed with an incoming call. I quickly silenced it and noticed the caller ID was the law firm Pete worked at. I exited from the side door and answered it once outside the building. "Sadie Sabatini."

"Hello, Ms. Sabatini, this is the secretary for attorney Joseph Thomas. Mr. Jensen has asked Mr. Thomas to represent you at the hearing on Friday. He would like to meet this afternoon to review all the details."

Though it was the last thing I wanted to do, it was important to ensure I had a backup plan–a.k.a. solid legal representation–should Plans A through G fall apart tomorrow night. "Of course, what time?"

"Three o'clock today at our offices. We're on the top floor of the Harness, Saddle, and Pierce building. Do you need the address?"

"No, I can find it. Is that in Crockett County?"

"No ma'am, Houston County."

"That presents a problem due to the ankle bracelet I'm wearing, courtesy of law enforcement in my county."

"I'll notify them, and they will grant a temporary waiver. You will have two hours before and two hours after the appointment."

"Sounds great, thank you."

Once at home, I checked all my email accounts. Thankfully, one was waiting for me from Jessica. She'd found the information necessary to locate my lost sheep–the person who had framed me with the text to Karen. I wrote down the numbers needed to ping the phone, and if all went well, lead me straight to the culprit. She also warned in the email she was pretty sure it was a burner phone so it might not be active anymore. I knew I would have discarded it by now, but one must at least try, right?

I thanked her and opened the program on my laptop to monitor the cellphone. Once turned on, the program would identify the location and send me the needed information. In my gut, I knew it had to be Natalie. The reason she only chose Karen to blackmail and not Jackie was one of the first questions I wanted to ask.

While online, I also logged into my cloud account for my security system. I was confident the motion sensors and video footage would prove I didn't leave my house in the wee hours of the morning to kill Miles. I was equally confident the footage would show that Dante had. Once I cleared my name, I would then find a way to help him. One problem at a time. I couldn't help anyone if I was locked up. The account opened and I clicked on the folder for the night in question.

It was empty.

That couldn't be right. Maybe it had been saved in a folder for the day previous or the day after. I clicked on both of those.

Empty.

It only took another minute or so of clicking for a

mini boulder to form in the pit of my stomach. Someone had gained access to my account and deleted not one day, not one week, but all the video files. This was not good. I didn't think Natalie's skill set included computer hacking, but maybe she'd picked up some tricks along the way. My heart clenched as I realized the more likely option was that Dante had been the one to do this dirty deed. He had the best access since he was inside my home. Perhaps, he had realized the footage would incriminate him and decided to remove that little obstacle from his path.

It was the most likely explanation, but I didn't like it. Not one bit.

There was nothing that could be done about it now.

My stomach rumbled, the pastry I'd eaten early this morning having all but disappeared. There was no time for food, so it would have to wait. After getting ready, it would be time to head over to the law firm. I needed a professional to tell me exactly what my chances were. Even without paying a retainer that would be drawn against at a rate of one hundred and eighty-nine dollars per hour (yes, I'd googled the average rate of criminal lawyers in Houston), I knew my chances weren't good.

The drive into Houston took just under two hours. I didn't expect it to be that bad this time of day as it wasn't a typical rush hour and most people should still be at work. The law firm was located in a beautifully landscaped area, which softened the fifteen-floor brick building and added to its look of prestige.

Once I provided the necessary information to the security guard on the main floor, I was granted access to the elevators that delivered me to the top floor. The barrier between those departing from the elevators and the receptionist was a wall of glass with a door that required you to be buzzed in.

I held up my visitor pass and was allowed entrance. To me, it felt like they were putting a lot of faith in the security on the first floor as a pass like this would not be hard to recreate, but I digressed.

"Good afternoon, how may I help you?"

"I have a three o'clock appointment with Joseph Thomas."

She handed me a clipboard with a form to fill out. "Please complete this. I'll let him know you are here."

I'd just completed the required documentation and wrote out the check (as instructed on the form) for the retainer when I heard Pete's voice. "Hey, Sadie, good to see you."

Standing, I extended my hand. "While seeing you here wouldn't be my first choice, I do appreciate that you connected me with Mr. Thomas."

"I understand. He's the best. Are you being a good girl and following all the rules of your parole?"

Since lying to him wasn't something I wanted to do, especially after he'd been so helpful, I decided to share what I assumed he wanted to hear. "I promise, no matter what happens, I'm going to make sure Kelsey gets her money back." Remembering what I'd learned earlier that day, I added, "I don't want her to miss out on any investment opportunities because of me."

His face scrunched up in what appeared to be confusion. "Not sure what you're talking about, but okay."

Maybe Pete didn't know that Kelsey was going to invest in Miles' business, either? It didn't seem likely. For all their fussing, they were a pretty solid couple who I didn't think hid things from one another. I guess you never knew these days. Regardless, I made a mental note to make sure the funds were transferred so I could write her a check. I'd put it in the mail before I left for the warehouse tomorrow night as the chances of me being successful were very slim. This translated to the strong probability of ending up in jail for violation of my parole.

"Is this other guy as good as you are?" It still made me nervous that a complete stranger would be representing me. "I really wish you were my attorney."

Pete sat down in the chair across from me. His gaze swept across the room before settling on me. "Trust me, you don't want me on your case. Criminal law is not my strength. You ever want to do a business or real estate deal, I'm your guy."

I studied him for a minute. "Something happened in the past, didn't it? Something that made you decide to leave criminal law behind."

"That's more of a weekend conversation complete with liquid courage."

Whatever had happened to Pete or his client in the past haunted him. I could see it in the clouds of his light blue eyes. Before I could ask anymore or share my concerns about Kelsey, I heard another voice.

"Oh, hi, Pete."

"Hey, JT." He stood and gestured for me to do the same. "This is Sadie Sabatini."

A middle-aged man of medium height and lean build smiled and shook my hand. "So, this is my three o'clock."

He had a nice, reassuring smile. His charcoal hair with matching moustache framed a tanned face. "Nice to meet you, Mr. Thomas. Pete has had nothing but good things to say about you. I appreciate you taking on my case."

"I paid Pete off to say nice things," he chuckled.

"Do you use top shelf tequila as payment like I do?"

"Hey, hey, you two. Enough talk about me. I think you have some work to do, don't you?" Pete teased.

I admit it was kind of fun, but since he'd been really helpful and on his best behavior, I'd play nice as well. "Seriously, Pete. I appreciate your help."

"That's what friends do. Now, I've got to run, but I'll catch up with you later."

I followed JT down a hall lined with modern artwork. His office matched the affluence and up-scale décor of the rest of the building. The name plaque next to his door read, *Joseph T. Thomas III, Esq.*

"Were your father and grandfather attorneys as

well?" I asked, easing into what would undoubtedly be a more difficult conversation.

He chuckled. "Yes, I come from a long line of attorneys. It was either that or ranching. I decided this was less work."

"Good call. I like having generational experience on my side." With a bunch of attorneys in one's family, I was sure dinner conversation probably centered around law strategy. Well, at least, I hoped it did.

"I assure you, you're in good hands. Come on in and have a seat. Let's get started."

Over the next several minutes, I reviewed the timeline from the moment of the altercation with Miles to my subsequent arrest a few days later. I finished with, "I was hoping my security camera footage would provide the proof needed to support my alibi of home, in bed, basically alone."

"You have security footage? Why didn't you just share that with the cops to begin with? It would have saved you a lot of time and money, not to mention avoiding the constant monitoring."

This was a harder question to answer, but I decided at this point, I would need to rely on the truth setting me free since technology had failed me. "I didn't share initially because I was worried it would incriminate my friend. By the time I decided to save myself before I saved him, the footage had been erased."

"Sounds to me like your friend was less worried about saving you than he was saving himself."

"Unfortunately, that does seem to be the case."

"Your friend have a history of violence? We can always put him forward as an alternate suspect to cast reasonable doubt."

"I don't really want to do that, for reasons I'm not willing to explain."

He leaned back in his leather, high-backed chair and steepled his fingers as he contemplated his next move. Or, maybe, he was trying to figure out a way to tell me how utterly stupid I was being. Regardless, I would be patient and wait. After several long moments, he leaned forward. "For now, I'll honor your request. But, Ms. Sabatini, I don't like to lose. So, if the time comes I feel it's necessary, I'll put you on the stand, ask about Dante, and if you refuse to cooperate, I'll treat you as a hostile witness."

Before I could respond, his features softened. "Please don't make me have to do that."

"I can't promise, but I hope it won't be necessary, either."

He nodded. "All right, in the interim, I'm going to reach out to the police station and the district attorney and request a copy of the coroner's report. I think it's high time we know what the true cause of death is, don't you?"

"That has been a question I've been wanting an answer to for days now. Thank you for wanting to get to the bottom of this as much as I do." My smile was one of relief.

JT laughed. "Well, it is what you pay me for. Stay

out of trouble and I'll work on your defense. With any luck, we can get this dismissed at your preliminary hearing on Friday. It's at eight-thirty in the morning. Please don't be late."

"Well, if I am," I lifted my pant leg and pointed at my accessory, "You'll know where to find me."

"Very funny." He tried to sound stern, but the smile on his face gave him away. Assuming I got out of this mess, JT the third would be my new attorney on retainer to handle all the messier aspects of my life.

I stood. "Thank you again for agreeing to represent me." I pulled the check out of my purse. "Should I leave this with you?"

He took the payment. "I'll give it to my admin. She'll email you a receipt."

Once back in the lobby, I noticed Pete had just finished up in the conference room. I stepped inside to say goodbye. "Hey. Pete, thanks again for connecting me with Mr. Thomas. I really appreciate it."

"Glad it worked out."

I hesitated for a second before deciding to ask Pete the question I wouldn't ask Kelsey right now. Though, I was certain he would tell her. "Can I ask you something?"

He stopped picking up and organizing the folders and papers surrounding him. "As long as it's not about why I don't practice criminal law, you can."

"I'll admit I'm curious, but that's not the question."

"Then shoot."

"Why didn't you or Kelsey tell me she was looking

to invest with Miles? Was she worried I would think she was a suspect?" It was a valid assumption as I'd put the rest of the potential investors in the possibly guilty category.

His face screwed up as he turned his attention fully on me. "What makes you think that?"

I sighed. "I might have been eavesdropping earlier today at The Club."

"And Kelsey said she was going to be an investor?"

Shaking my head, I confirmed, "No."

"Did you ask her?"

The head shaking continued. "No."

"I don't get women." He sighed. "You two are supposedly best friends, but you won't just ask her a simple question?"

"I have my reasons."

He picked up all the paperwork and moved toward the door. "Well, I have my reasons for not answering your question. You want to know. You ask her."

"Fair enough."

And with that, he was gone. I turned in my visitor badge downstairs and headed home. During the drive, my phone dinged. At a stoplight, I checked to see it was a notification from the messaging board. My off-the-wall phrase to convince Dante to meet me this evening had been read. There was no way to know by whom, but hope was a wonderful thing. It's certainly better than the alternative.

Traffic was just starting to build to normal rush hour as I made my way down I-45. Barring any accidents, I would make it back into my county in plenty of time. The sun would be setting within thirty minutes of my arrival home, so there needed to be no delays. Darkness came early this time of year. While meeting Dante under the cover of night didn't concern me, I was more worried he would think I wasn't going to show if I didn't get there in a timely manner. The question remained, though. Would Natalie be with him? And, if not, how would I convince him to take my side over hers? I hated it had to be that way, but the battle lines had been drawn.

Tonight, I would know whether Plan A was going to work, or worst case scenario, we needed to jump straight to Plan F, which would not be good. Because Plan F meant I failed.

Chapter Fourteen

I'd managed a quick sandwich and had settled on the back deck with a glass of wine just as the sun was setting. One sip in, I heard his voice. "That was pretty risky."

"Does Nat know you're here?"

"No."

Whew, we weren't jumping ahead to the immediate failure of all my plans. "Then, it was just the right amount of risk." He moved into my line of sight before sitting down in the chair next to me. His gaze focused on the orange sun dissolving into the water. "You want a beer or something else to drink?"

"No."

"I figured out what you meant by the zig zag job. I just can't figure out if someone has been trying to zig me while I'm zagging or if it's you pulling the strings."

"Whose strings do you think I've been pulling?"

I sighed. "I'm hoping it's Natalie's and not mine, otherwise I've totally misread you and this situation."

He graced me with a smile. "You always were the smart one. I owe you my life many times over."

His words sobered me, even though I experienced a small measure of relief that he had been pulling the bait and switch on Natalie rather than me. "So, why did you help her frame me?"

Dante's gaze shifted away from the sky to his lap. "I wanted her to find peace. She's been so messed up since we split."

"I'm so sorry. It felt safer for us to part ways. We were spending more time running to safety than helping others."

"Yeah, I know. She just had unfinished business."

"Miles."

"Yeah, but she went too far. That's why I'm here."

"It's going to be hard for me to help her and you if I'm sitting in jail for a crime I didn't commit."

"Like I said, you're smart. You'll figure it out."

This wasn't getting me anywhere. "Well, I do have a plan, but it might upset Natalie. Do you know she has plans to destroy Miles' research facility, both the good research and the bad?"

"Again, that's why I'm here. I need you to stop that. And stop her."

"I'm going to do my best, but I hope you realize I'm putting my freedom on the line."

"I know. There ain't no other way."

Oh, I could think of lots of ways to take Miles and

his research down that would be easier. But that ship had sailed, so there was no need to ponder on what could have been. We had to focus on what was now and what would be. "Did you or Natalie kill Miles?"

"No."

"So, you took my knife and erased my security footage?"

"No, and Nat didn't, either. Well, yes to the knife, no to the footage."

I could tell there was more to the story. "But?"

He sighed. "But she convinced Jessica to do it."

My gaze snapped to him, and I was certain my eyes were blazing. "Jessica betrayed me, too?"

"Only because she thought she was protecting me. Nat told her I snuck out to kill Miles for her and she needed the proof of that gone."

Wow, Natalie hadn't just gone down the wrong path, she'd dragged Dante and Jessica along with her. "Why did she try to frame me for blackmailing Karen?"

Dante stood abruptly, knocking the chair back several feet. "I don't know how else to explain it to you. She's out for revenge. She saw you leading a good life, and Miles out doing what he did before and creating the potential to hurt so many people. Vengeance on both of you became her only goal."

He started pacing and I took a couple steps back to stay out of his path. "When she was just after Miles, I was game to play along. I hated that dude, too, but not as much as she did. We tracked him from California to

Texas, and it was just dumb luck we learned both of you were in the same town."

"That doesn't feel like luck."

And that's when I knew it wasn't. Miles had located me and inserted himself into my life. He wanted to make me pay for what I'd done to him. I'm sure if someone hadn't killed him, he would have worked hard to make my life a living hell. Of course, in death, he was doing a pretty good job of it, too.

He stopped. "Yeah, no such thing as coincidence."

"No, sir, there isn't."

"What a mess."

He wasn't wrong. This was a mess. "I need you to keep Nat busy tomorrow night. Keep her away from the warehouse. I'm going to try to stop it from being destroyed, and I can't do that if I'm worried about her showing up and taking her frustration out on me. Oh, by the way, I'm not really appreciating the skills you've shared with her. I've already found myself looking up at her from the ground thanks to that."

Dante merely shrugged. Just as well, I probably wouldn't buy what he was selling, anyway. "Anything else I should know? I'm pretty wiped out. It's been a long day."

He pulled me into a big, beautiful bear hug. I felt warm, and for a moment, safe from the craziness of life. I blinked back tears at the thought of how different things were now from a little over a year ago. Instead of a team, there was revenge, blackmail, and conspiracies at every turn. I needed to fix it. I just didn't know how.

My breath stuttered as I let it out before pulling away. "Thanks. I needed that."

"I know it doesn't seem like it right now, but I've got your six. Always have. Always will."

Before I could say anything, he disappeared into the darkness.

I'd just finished a long, hot shower and made it into my nightclothes when the front doorbell rang. I checked the security camera, worried that it would be the police again. Maybe Natalie had managed to frame me for something else. Instead, it was Kelsey. She didn't look happy.

The moment the door opened, she crossed her arms and her green eyes blazed. "Help me understand why you thought it was okay to ask Pete things you should have been asking me."

I opened my mouth to respond, but she continued. "And eavesdropping? Really, Sadie?"

My second attempt to speak was thwarted as well. "Then, you apparently left before you heard the rest of the story. And in case you're wondering, that side of the story would be my part. Right now, you only have your interpretation of Dora Lee's side. Since when do you pay her any attention?"

Giving her a few extra seconds to see if she had any more to say, I offered a crooked grin. "Can I talk now?"

Her visage softened and a small smile crept onto her face. "Only if you invite me in."

Stepping aside, I gestured to the couch. "Please." I

followed her into the room. "Wine or something to drink?"

"I don't guess after my tirade a moment ago, you'd make me a decaf cappuccino, would you?"

I chuckled. "Of course. And because you were pretty spot on with your tirade, I'll even add some sugar free vanilla, just the way you like it."

"Thanks."

Once we both had our drinks, I sat in the chair across from her. Even though I'd admitted there was some truth to her assessment from earlier today, I figured it couldn't hurt to start with an apology. "For what it's worth, I'm sorry I spied on you earlier today and even sorrier I asked Pete something I should have talked to you about. In my defense, he was there and you weren't when the question was burning a hole in my brain."

She sighed. "What do you want to know?"

There were several things, but one had created a bigger hole than the rest. "Do you feel I've betrayed you?"

Her gaze narrowed. "What makes you think I feel that way?"

I shrugged. "You didn't correct Dora Lee when she said it."

Her cup was carefully placed on the end table next to the couch before she crossed her arms. For the record, that was never a good sign. "Have you experienced success with convincing the matriarch of the

Birmingham family that she was wrong at any point in your dealings with her?"

And my head began shaking again. Too much more of this and I was going to have the mother of all headaches to contend with tonight. I sighed. "No, I haven't. Should I apologize again?"

Kelsey chuckled. "Not necessary. If you would've stuck around a little longer, you would've heard me set her on the straight and narrow path."

"Now, I'm mad I missed that. A call from my attorney forced me to move outside. Did she admit she was wrong?"

"What do you think?"

"Not a chance, but I bet it felt good to at least watch her face turn red."

The chuckling turned to all out laughter. "A bit."

As the humor died down, I figured it was as good a time as any to ask another question. "Why didn't you tell me you wanted to invest in Miles' business?"

She picked up her drink and took another sip. "Because I didn't."

"But Dora Lee said..."

The arching eyebrow was my signal to stop that train of thought. "Dora Lee was misinformed."

"Ugh, I really screwed this one up. I should've known better."

She moved over to sit next to me, resting her hand on my knee. "Yes, you should have. My potential investment opportunity is with James Cutter. He'd reached out to Ted asking if he could connect him with someone outside of his family's accountants and investment brokers who could help him manage a large portfolio."

"So, Ted told his mom, I'm sure, in a moment of pride about connecting an employee of his bank with Mr. Cutter."

"Exactly. Ted couldn't help but tout that detail to Dora Lee, even though we still have about ten days before our appointment. For whatever reason, she seems to think James' investing was dependent on his deal with Miles."

"That doesn't make any sense."

"Agreed."

We both sat in silence for several minutes, contemplating this information. I pulled out the notes I'd made since this whole crazy thing started about a week ago. "I wrote down that James was going to potentially invest more in Miles' venture in a little over thirty days from the initial investment. That would take us to the first of next week, about five days before he was going to meet with you about investing, isn't it?"

"Yes, that sounds about right."

"What was going to happen after that thirty-day mark that James was waiting on? I mean, he's part of the Cutter family. They have about as much money as the good Lord, or at least the Birminghams. So, why the wait?"

Kelsey yawned and stood up. "That, my friend, is apparently one of life's greatest questions right now."

"Ugh, I'm really tired of all these pieces not fitting together nice and neat."

"Get some sleep. It will come to you."

"I hope you're right." I walked her to the door and gave her a hug goodnight. "Thanks for being the best friend I have here in Wilson and for coming over here so I could make things right. For what it's worth, I was going to come to the bank first thing tomorrow morning."

"You didn't have an appointment," she teased.

"Oh, I was arriving as a walk-in and would have just sat outside your door until you agreed to see me."

Kelsey laughed. "Well, I'm glad it didn't come to that. Can't have you making a scene and getting Ted involved."

"I don't know, think of the fun stories Dora Lee would tell at mahjong with those juicy details."

"You're incorrigible."

"Yeah, but you love me just like I am."

She nodded. "Goodnight, Sadie."

"Goodnight, Kelsey."

Before turning in for the night, I sent a message to my father's work email. I knew he didn't check them after a certain time, and I didn't want to wake him. He would see it first thing in the morning and would reply, hopefully, with the information I needed. Even though it was quarter end, I was hoping he'd had time to look into the Cutter Cares foundation I'd asked him about.

With thoughts of the Cutter millions cluttering my mind, I drifted off into a restless sleep.

* * *

Since I didn't have to stage a sit-in at the bank this morning, I decided to spend what might be my last day of freedom at Tesoro. The first thing I did was check the status of my safe. Everything appeared to be in order and accounted for. Walking over to the jewelry section, I picked out a pair of earrings that would complement the dark auburn of Kelsey's hair and the light green of her eyes. Call it a peace offering or friendship gift. Whatever it was, she'd earned it over the past week.

Before I headed back to the counter to wrap it up for her, my gaze caught another piece. This one was a necklace, but the glass had been formed into swirls intertwined one with another. It made me think of Nat. I picked it up with the intention of wrapping it and giving it to her once all of this was over. This would serve as my peace offering to her.

As I'd tossed and turned last night, I realized that maybe a clean break for the team hadn't been the best way to handle our situation. We'd been together, night and day, through thick and thin covering for each other for over ten years. Going from having a support system like that to being on your own, cold turkey, wasn't an easy thing to do. Guilt reasserted itself in a fierce way. It was especially unfair for my team. They'd followed my lead the whole time and entrusted me to keep them safe. I'd left them out there without a safety net.

All of this was on me.

Once the gifts were wrapped, I picked up my cell and opened an encrypted line. I dialed Jessica's number. "Who's calling?"

"It's me, Jess. It's Sadie."

There was a long pause. "Is everything all right?"

"No, it's not. I'm calling to tell you I'm sorry."

"I'm the one who's sorry. You probably know by now about the security footage. I shouldn't have violated your trust by helping Natalie out. I was just worried about Dante. I didn't realize–"

"That she was using you so I wouldn't have the ability to prove my innocence?"

"Yeah. That."

"It's okay. She used you like she's been using him. But I'm going to try and fix all of this. And once I do, we're all going to get together in a safe place and talk through how to let go of our past, but still support each other in the future. It was unfair of me to ask so much of all of you."

"Don't blame yourself for any of this. You protected us for over ten years and gave us all the tools we needed to keep ourselves safe for the future. The fact that Nat chose to ignore all of it to carry out her revenge on Miles, well, that's on her, not you."

I appreciated her words, but I still felt responsible. "Either way, what's done is done. All that remains is to fix it and move forward."

"I do miss you, though."

My tears had to be blinked back to prevent them

escaping. "I miss you, too. We'll get together soon. Promise."

"Stay safe, Sadie, and be smart."

"You too, my friend. You too."

The rest of the day passed by in a blur. The customers were almost non-stop. I figured it was either curiosity over the woman suspected of murder, or as I preferred to see it, people had been sad I was closed several days in a row and were now coming in to make their purchases. It had been a record sales day.

Once at home, I made myself a nice dinner and had a glass of my favorite wine. I watched the sun set over the lake as I made my final plans for the evening. The goal was to stop the lab from being destroyed. It was important that the good research be allowed to continue and the bad be safely dealt with so no one else would have the opportunity to use it. Since I would have no way of knowing which was which, that meant it all had to be saved until it could be sorted out. I would entrust James Cutter to see that the good in all of this did not disappear.

I pulled out my laptop and cast my votes for the board. Just in case things went terribly wrong tonight, I wanted to show my support for those I chose to lead Wilson into the future. While the browser tab was open, I also researched ways to remove my ankle bracelet. Sadly, there didn't seem to be a safe way to do it other than the normal legal procedures. Since the only time frame I had to work with was before midnight, that made planning this job to take place in less than twenty minutes, and allowing for the five minutes to get there and the five for the return trip, highly unlikely. My only hope was that I could accomplish my mission and stop the bad guys before the police arrived to arrest me. The percentage of success—well, that number was too low to focus on.

If it were any other situation, I'd abandon the plan and wait for a better time. But my hearing was tomorrow morning, and unless the cause of death angle came through, there was little chance I wouldn't at least have to wait out the rest of my pre-trial and trial days in a locked cell. If I got arrested tonight, it was just one more night to add to however many I already had to do, so it was a calculated risk I was willing to take.

I did a quick walkthrough of my home and made sure any evidence of my past had been hidden or removed. Fingerprints had been dutifully wiped clean since I no longer could be sure that Dante or Natalie hadn't been in the house without my knowledge. My security system was good, but Natalie was better, and the video footage was gone.

At ten-thirty, donned all in black, I bid my house and neighborhood goodbye and headed toward the warehouse. This was it. My future rested on whatever happened over the next ninety minutes. The odds were definitely not in my favor, but that had never stopped me before, and certainly wasn't going to tonight.

The drive to the county line was made without incident. I set an alarm for thirty minutes and made sure the alert was only a vibration. No need to clue someone to my presence if I happened to still be there when time elapsed. I checked my inbox one final time to see if my father had emailed me. Nothing. Oh well, I guess my curiosity about Cutter Cares and its mission would have to wait.

Less than five minutes later, I pulled into the parking lot. Carefully avoiding any well-lit areas, I backed into the space and moved toward the building under the cover of darkness. I saw two other vehicles. That could mean it would be two against one, or if those vehicles had the maximum number of passengers...well, there was no point in thinking about those odds.

The lock was picked reasonably fast given the amount of perspiration and shaking of my hands. I opened the door quietly, ignoring the pounding of my heart. A quick peek inside revealed the hallway toward the office was empty. My plan was to get into the cabinet I couldn't the other day, take pictures of any incriminating evidence, and then find whoever was going to destroy the research and stop them. Easy peasy, right?

Thankfully, the office door wasn't locked. That detail concerned me, but not enough to dissuade me from my objective. Once inside, I slipped a headband on that contained a small muted light. Again, it was important to see, but I didn't want anyone to see light under the door as they walked by when there should be darkness. The lock on the filing cabinet proved not to be a challenge. My fingers moved over each folder tab, looking for something–anything–that would help. Everything from building permits to personnel files were in the top drawer. I quickly took a picture of the names on each folder. It may come in handy in the future. The second drawer contained financial papers. I pulled those out and started laying them on the desk, snapping pictures and scanning them with my eyes at the same time.

My activity stopped as I reviewed the information under capital income and expenditures. As expected, James Cutter had made a reasonably sized investment. Under the future/expected column, there were five names: James Cutter, followed by a number with a lot of zeros and a date that implied cash was expected in the next week. While it still didn't answer the question of why the delay, it confirmed my suspicions. The next three names weren't a surprise: Karen Bizzy, JB Nester, and Ted Birmingham. While not as many zeros as the Cutter number, there were still enough to reflect the access to wealth they each had. There was one more entry, though, that gave me pause. There, in black and white, was another name. A person who, when I thought back, had ensured my focus was on someone else. This individual had the means and the opportunity, but no motive I could think of at the moment. Someone who possessed the ability to entice Miles out of his home in the wee hours of the morning.

That someone was none other than Estelle (EZ) Zimmerman.

Chapter Fifteen

While I wanted to give thought as to why EZ might have killed Miles, it would have to wait until later. The fact she kept the detail that she was also a potential investor from me caused alarm, but thinking her capable of killing someone...

Well, I had no time to think about that right now.

Placing the folder back in the drawer, I continued my search. My phone buzzed, and while the temptation to ignore it was great, my need to know demanded I at least look. It was an email from my father. I guess quarter end had him up late as well. Opening the email, I scanned the message in a quest to get right to the heart of the matter. There, in black and white, was the answer to at least one question that had been bugging me:

Sadie, I finally had a moment to email you what I learned about the Cutter Cares legacy and family. Each heir receives a million dollars annually starting on their thirtieth birthday. However, seventy-five percent of the money is earmarked and can only be used as an investment in or for support of a worthy cause that is approved by the board. If they fail to do so, they lose access to that money and the Cutter fortune. It's their way of making sure their legacy lives on. It appears your man, James Cutter, has had several failed attempts to find a business that meets the family requirements. Hope this helps. Love, Dad

I quickly googled James Cutter to see if I could find out when his birthday was. My gut told me it had to be soon. That would explain so much of his reactions I'd witnessed over the past week. It took more clicks and time than I really wanted to give to the quest, but now that I'd started, I needed to know. Finally, I found the birthdate of one James Cutter.

It was next week.

The light to the office clicked on, and my adrenaline spiked. "See anything interesting?"

My heart stopped for a moment as I recognized the voice. I was angry at myself for being so distracted that I hadn't heard anyone come in. After a calming breath, I turned and smiled. "Only that your birthday is coming up in a few days. Happy early birthday, Mr. Cutter."

In response, James grinned, but the smile didn't reach his eyes. Which, in case you were wondering, was an indicator it was totally fake. "It was going to be a great birthday until your old friend decided to pull a fast one on me and use my money for revenge on his former company. Oh, and I'm pretty sure you were on the list of people he wanted to destroy as well."

The words he said barely registered as most of my focus was on the gun he held in his all too steady hand. Most notably, I recognized the silencer screwed on to the end of the barrel. If he killed me, no one would even hear the shot. Not that there was any human life within a mile of our location. How could I call for help?

I shifted my feet, trying to dispel some of the nervous energy pulsing through my system. The weight on my right ankle reminded me. My ankle bracelet! Earlier, the fear of not being out of here in the allotted time was a huge concern. Oddly enough, now it could be my salvation. If I kept him talking for another fifteen or twenty minutes, my ankle bracelet would hopefully send an alert to law enforcement. I would be arrested for violation of my parole, but that was preferable over being dead. Of course, I also remembered that I'd surmised there was a grace period built in since I didn't get arrested the first time I'd violated those rules.

My phone buzzed again, and I couldn't help but look. The program I had running in the background to ping Natalie's location if she turned on the burner phone had done its job. I wasn't sure whether to be relieved or worried that the program identified her as very near my location. Depending on whose side she came down on, this could be very good news, or more likely, very bad. I guess my plea to Dante to keep her busy tonight and away from here didn't work. Perhaps, I'd been the one he was running the zig zag job on all along. If so, he'd done it masterfully.

"Give me the phone. You won't be needing it any longer."

Before handing it over, I locked the screen. Mine required a passcode rather than facial recognition or a fingerprint. Those were too easy to get from people who were incapacitated for one reason or the other—like being dead. "I know why I'm here so late, how about you?"

"I'm here because of you." His voice was calm and steady.

I did not see that coming. "Me?"

"Follow me." He gestured toward the door with the barrel of the gun. As I had no options, I complied. We exited the office, and he turned off the light. Very smart if he was trying to avoid anyone knowing we were here. We walked down the long hall to the end. He opened the door like a true gentleman. Ironic, under the circumstances, but manners were manners, I suppose.

My headlamp illuminated the area, revealing a lab with various test tubes and equipment throughout. The workstations were in two equal rows. Given what I'd learned, most likely one side was for Product A and the other for Product B. I felt his grip on my biceps as he led me to the corner. There was a second set of light switches on the wall, near which he positioned us so he would be close enough to turn them on or off. If that was important, I had no idea. "Once our guests arrive, one word out of you and it's permanently lights out. Understood?

"Understood."

"Turn off your headlamp."

Being near the switches made a little more sense now. I really didn't want to plunge us into total darkness, but the gun trumped anything I wanted. I complied and we stood together, his hand on my arm, shrouded in the shadows. While we waited for whatever or whoever, I decided it was a good time to ask questions to validate my theories. Again, buying time was crucial. "Were you the one who framed me for Miles' murder?" Maybe it was why he said he was here because of me?

He chuckled. "No, that was just a beautiful gift someone unknowingly laid at my feet."

Great, that meant it really was one of my team members. Since the chances of me making my hearing and learning the true cause of death were dwindling by the minute, I asked, "Why did you kill him? How?"

"You know if I tell you that, there's no way you can leave here alive."

This time I chuckled, though it was born out of fear rather than humor. "I'll be honest, I didn't think that was a possibility, anyway."

The silence stretched longer than I cared for. Maybe he hadn't really thought this all the way through. My presence here was possibly not part of his plan. Perhaps, the gun was more of a deterrent for whoever was going to try to destroy the research. Since he wasn't talking, might as well continue to share my thoughts. "Let me see how much I can figure out while we wait."

Silence ensued, so I continued. "You believed Miles when he sold you the idea of drought resistant plants. As you were running out of time to find a worthy project under Cutter Cares to invest your early inheritance in, it wasn't a hard sell for him. You made the initial investment but knew once the board reviewed all the information and financials, you would be good as gold. Except, somehow you learned Miles had duplicitous intentions. Which, for what it's worth, proper research would have revealed he'd done this before."

The grip on my arm tightened. "I suggest you watch your words and tone."

This would have been the perfect opportunity to tell him I couldn't watch my words in the darkness he'd plunged us into, but the more rational side of my brain won out over the sass. Instead, I tried logic. "I get it. He took advantage of your situation." I figured that was better phrasing than, "He conned you." Those words would prematurely end my life, I suspected.

"He wouldn't provide the paperwork and financials needed for me to get the approval."

"You learned that on Friday night at The Club, didn't you?"

"Yes." He ground out the word, anger lacing his tone. "And thanks to your antics at dinner, it made me start to question him and his motives."

Ah, so my comments had started this whole thing. Maybe that's what he'd meant by being here because of me. "Did you come here and find paperwork to prove what he was up to?"

"I didn't have to. Images of the proof were sent to my phone. That was enough for me."

"Any idea who sent them?" Though, I had a pretty good idea.

"No, and I didn't care. Once I saw the images, I got angrier and angrier with each passing hour. I went to confront him."

That explained why Miles came outside in the wee hours of the morning and guided them to the wooded area. He wanted to talk his way out of his predicament without anyone overhearing. "As he's now dead, it's reasonable to assume he did not successfully convince you his intentions were one hundred percent honorable."

"Oh, he tried, but I'm not stupid."

I could debate that with him, but what was the point? "Why not just turn him in? You had the proof. You could have sent him to jail for a long time."

The grip was now so tight I feared there would be bruises. Finally, he spoke. "He laughed at me and told me we needed each other. He needed my money, and I needed to secure my inheritance." His voice was deep and strained, indicating to me he was barely holding it together.

"That's right. This was your last chance. If you didn't get approval from the board, you would be essentially cut out of the will and all the money would be gone. Though, once news hit that a large agriculture company had been ruined by your pet project, I'm thinking the board would have revoked your access to future funds."

The vibrating alarm went off on my watch. I'd managed to stay alive in the hopes of being rescued and arrested. I tapped my watch to turn off the alarm.

"What was that?"

"Just a reminder to take my nighttime meds," I lied.

"You're going to miss them tonight."

"So, how did you kill him?" I really, really wanted to know.

Before he could answer, voices were heard outside the door. "One word..."

I remained silent. There was no need to say one word to confirm my understanding. The door opened and someone came in, holding a flashlight. They were followed by another person. Thanks to the darkness, I couldn't determine if I knew either one of them. The first person spoke. "I don't think a fire is the best way to do this. If emergency vehicles are dispatched, they could put it out before everything is destroyed."

"We're in the middle of nowhere. Who's going to call in the fire department? By the time anyone notices, it will be too late. We've already hit the office, all that's left is the lab."

Oh great, now there was not only a gun to threaten my life, but a fire had been started in the building. I ran through all the contingency plans in my head. It only took a few seconds to realize I'd not planned for being held hostage by a man with a gun and two additional people present with the intent to set a fire. Yup, that took me straight through the entire alphabet and to Ground Zero. Survival was the key now.

"You set this on fire, and I'll kill you both." James' firm voice cut through the darkness.

Okay, so maybe he was going to help me with the staying alive part. Well, at least I wouldn't die a horrible death starting with smoke inhalation and ending with–yeah, I wasn't going to go there.

The light behind me flipped on, and the other two in the room came into view. The man, I didn't know. As the other person was Natalie, it was safe to assume he was the person she'd hired to destroy the evidence. She obviously didn't have a lot of faith he was going to do as she asked since she was here, too.

"Hey, Sadie."

Under instructions not to utter one word, I simply nodded.

"You know these people?" James used the grip on my arm to pull me forward and in front of him. I really disliked being used as a human shield.

"I know her, not him."

"What plan are you on?" Nat asked.

"Oh, I'm at the end, for sure." But then, a thought struck me. If I could count on Nat being on my side for even a few minutes, we both might make it out of here alive. "It's time to accept the odds." I prayed she remembered those code words.

"Both of you, shut up! I need to think." James pressed the barrel of the gun to my forehead. I did my best to not let fear show on my face, but my heart pounded harder than a bass drum and adrenaline began to course through my veins like fire.

My gaze fixed on Nat's. I needed to see if she was happy I might die or if there still might be a chance for us to fix this. Time to find out. I stepped slightly to the side, not enough to cause James alarm, but enough to kick my final plan into motion. With a long inhale and exhale of breath, I brought my arm up and swung it backwards with all the power I had inside of me. My target—James' groin.

The moment my fist hit his man parts, he cried out in pain, causing the gun to move away from my head and his grip to loosen. I ran toward the door, praying Natalie and the other guy would follow. I'd just made it outside the lab when a bullet hit the wall next to me. I risked a quick look back to see the other two right behind me. James' shot had missed. Pain could affect aim, for sure.

Smoke filled the hallway from the fire burning over the last several minutes while we were in the lab. My lungs burned, but I was more worried we wouldn't make it outside before James recovered. "In here!" The loudly whispered instruction forced me to turn toward the voice. It was the lab guy. Having no reason not to comply, I followed him and Nat into the room, which turned out to be a supply closet. He grabbed some shop cloths and stuffed them in the gap at the bottom of the door to minimize the amount of smoke allowed in.

"Great idea," I whispered, avoiding the thought that those cloths were not going to stop the fire once it reached us. We were now effectively trapped.

"Yeah, thanks, Norm," Nat whispered.

We waited a moment to see if James would be able to locate us. When nothing happened, I wanted to feel relief, but the fact he hadn't opened every door to look for us worried me. I shot a look at Nat and saw the same concern etched on her features as well.

"How long should we wait?" Nat whispered to Norm.

"Just long enough for you to send me the same images and proof you sent to James." His smirk told me we'd just been double crossed. Wow, if I made it out of this alive, I was going to brush up on my contingency planning. I'd missed this one by a landslide.

"You're working with James, aren't you?" More pieces clicked into place. I only wished I'd put it all together sooner.

Norm kept his gaze on Nat, but he answered me. "It's a recent development, yes. I don't know what his plans are, but I want to make something good out of the evil Miles planned here. Nat can help make that happen by sending me the pictures of the research."

"Did he make you aware that he murdered his last partner?" I figured I had nothing to lose at this point. My life was already hanging on by a very thin thread. One that would be on fire soon.

Alarm painted his features, but he held strong. "If I have the research, I can continue the work without him."

"You're unarmed and in the same fire trap we are. Your plan is as bad as hers," Nat pointed out.

Reaching behind him, he pulled a small, rectangular implement out of its hiding place, tucked in the back of his pants. "I think a taser qualifies, don't you?"

I wasn't sure how Nat felt about this, but avoiding electricity coursing through my nervous system just became a priority. I also knew if he deployed it, only one of us would be temporarily disabled. The initial assault would last about thirty seconds before he could reload another cartridge. One of us could try to render him incapable of delivering a second shot. It wasn't much, but it was all we had. I nodded. "Definitely qualifies."

"Now, send me the research," he directed to Nat. "I'm tired of playing around."

Time was running out. If Norm was working with James, he would be waiting somewhere with the gun to finish us off, whether Nat sent the research or not. And I was pretty sure she wasn't going to do that. I needed to say one last thing to her before I risked it all to save us both. "I'm so sorry for the pain I caused you. Sorry that you didn't feel like you could come to me so we could work all of this out together."

Her gaze bore into me, conflicted and hurt. There was so much we needed to set right. I prayed we would survive so we could fix it. I grabbed her hand and squeezed. "May the odds be ever in your favor."

Recognition dawned in her eyes as soon as I uttered the final code words of the night right before Norm yelled, "Give me your phone! I don't need you, just the data."

It was now or never. I lunged toward Norm, knocking him to the floor. The taser flew out of his grip and landed a few feet away. "Run!" I yelled to Nat.

She scooped up the taser and headed out into the thick, black smoke. Using the moves on Norm that Nat had skillfully demonstrated to me a few days ago, he found himself looking up at me as I straddled him. "We need to get out of here. Do you want to live or die?"

"Live." He coughed out his answer as the acrid air filled our lungs.

"Then, let's go. Stay low." I moved off him and crawled into the hallway. The sound of a gun firing made my heart lurch and quickened my pace. "Nat!" I screamed, the word strangled by my fear.

Ignoring everything else, I knew I needed to get to her. I stood and ran in the direction of the exit. With each step, my lungs burned until my breath only came in coughs. Darkness had filled the long space between me and the exit. Reaching up, I clicked the light on my headband, hoping it would be helpful. It wasn't much, but it got me to the wall. My hand kept in contact with the surface until it reached the corner, guiding me to where the door should be just to my left.

I pushed hard on the bar, making me fall forward.

"Nat! Where are you?" I no longer cared about the research, about James, about Norm, or about the fire. I needed to get to her to make sure she was all right.

The night sky did very little to illuminate the area. "Natalie, please!"

"Over here," a weak voice cried out.

I ran in the direction of the voice and found her lying on the ground, blood seeping out of the area under her left shoulder. I tried not to think about how close it was to her heart. I wanted to call for help, but James had taken my cell. "Do you still have your phone?"

Her head shook. "James took it after I tackled him. With the gun knocked out of his hand, I thought it would be a fair fight, but he had another gun."

All this effort and he was going to get away. I pulled her into my lap and pressed hard on the wound to try and stop the bleeding. "I'm so sorry, Sadie."

"Shhh, you're alive, and that's the most important part right now. It gives us a chance to talk through everything and set things straight between us."

The tears rolling down her cheeks glistened in the light of my headlamp. "It was me," she confessed.

"You what?" I didn't want her to waste energy on talking, but she was intent.

"I framed you. I was so mad..." Her body started shaking with her sobs.

"Hey, hey. I get it. I should have listened to you more. We should have finished the job completely." I smiled gently. "And once you're recovered, I need you to explain why you only blackmailed Karen and not Jackie."

"Family," she coughed.

"What?"

"That brother of hers is an idiot. I wasn't going to have him betray his own sister."

That actually made sense coming from Nat. "I get it. Family is everything to you."

She shook her head. "I was too close to the last situation. Couldn't see past the hate and my need for vengeance for what he did to my family, to all those people."

"And I should have realized that. I let you down." I hung my head. "I've let everyone down."

"Dante never stopped believing in you. He hated every second of my plotting against you."

"Where is he? I figured he would be close by." We really could use his help right now.

"He was monitoring the perimeter."

The fact he hadn't rushed in when the gunshot was heard now made me worry about his safety. Had James gotten to him, too? I'd only heard one shot, but my mind had been focused only on getting to Nat.

A moment later, sirens blared as police cars pulled into the lot. Sheriff vehicles and a fire truck followed closely behind. As soon as the car stopped, Jeremy jumped out. "Sadie!"

"Over here."

A moment later, he was by my side. He saw Nat's condition and yelled, "We need a medic over here."

They whisked Nat away, her hand finally being tugged from my grasp. Jeremy pulled me into his arms. "Are you okay?"

I shook my head and fought back tears, "No, not at all. The bad guys got away, Nat has been shot, I'm going to jail for violating my parole, and without any proof of James confessing to killing Miles, it was all for nothing."

"Hey, hey, that's not the Sadie I know. She's an optimist."

Looking up at him, I frowned. "I used to be, but the past week has sucked the optimism right out of me."

He smiled as his hand cupped my face. "Would it help to know that this law enforcement team wasn't the only one with me? The other caught a man fleeing from the scene, wielding a weapon. They now have him in custody."

For the first time in a week, a small glimpse of hope peeked in through the darkness. "It helps if that man in custody happens to be James Cutter."

His thumb brushed away some of the errant tears. "It is."

My arms circled his waist and I pulled him closer. "Any chance they also caught a guy in a lab coat making a getaway?"

He laughed. "They might have found one of those, too. They weren't sure if he was guilty or not, but figured he would know something."

"Oh, he knows a thing or two." I squeezed him tighter. "Thank you. Even though I know it was my ankle bracelet that called in the troops, I'm really glad you decided to join them."

"It was your ankle bracelet, but not in the way you think."

"Oh?"

"After our conversation the other day when you shared you were going to try to set things right from your past on Thursday night, it got me thinking,"

"And?" Now that I knew James and Norm were in custody and Nat was being tended to, I could shift my focus to Jeremy and how he came to be here. He might have arrived a little late to the party, but he was here and that's what mattered.

"When I thought back to what you said, I realized you were there to see if they were going to arrest you for violating your parole. I called in a favor with my buddy, and he pulled up the GPS signal on your device. We saw you had been outside the county line for about thirty-two minutes."

"More like thirty-one, but go on," I teased, feeling better than I had in days.

He returned my smile. "Well, the sheriff system says thirty-two, so that's what we'll go with. Anyway, I noted that a large portion of that time was spent here. It took all my powers of persuasion to convince them something was going to go down here tonight. Once they pulled up your location and realized you were at the same warehouse as before, I called in all my favors and rallied the troops."

I pulled back a bit. "Wait, so am I hearing you're

not above bending the rules to help someone who might be in trouble?"

His head shook, but the smile on his face told me he knew there was a bit of teasing in there. "You did violate your parole, so I'm not technically bending the rules."

"Mmhmm. Except, you had them pull up the information before the alarm went off. That's the only way you could have arrived when you did."

"Tomato, to-mah-tow. I'm here, and that's what counts."

"You know what counts the most?" I asked as I pulled him close again.

"What?"

"That your willingness to bend the line between right and wrong to help someone tells me that maybe we're not as far apart as we might have thought."

"Is that so?"

I held both sides of his face as I leaned in and kissed him. The feel of his arms tightening around me washed away all the angst of the past twenty-four hours. Maybe even a little farther back than that. After just enough time, I leaned my head back and smiled. "Yes, sir. That is so."

Epilogue

By Friday afternoon, it was all over. My attorney had used the coroner's report, which had finally been made available to him, to prove that Miles had died from poisoning. They found a puncture wound inside the bruising that remained from Dante's beating and the toxicology report confirmed it.

Nat had made a surprise appearance at my court hearing as well. She was in a wheelchair with Dante right beside her. She'd confessed to using my knife to stab Miles to frame me. Dante had admitted to stealing said knife. For their trouble, the judge sentenced Natalie to six months in jail, the minimum for such an offense, and Dante was fined five hundred dollars for the theft.

The charges against me were dropped, however, I did have to pay a penalty for violating my parole... twice. It was a small price to pay. Before they could take Nat away, I asked for a word with her. They gave me a few minutes.

"I'm going to come visit you every week," I promised. "We're going to talk through things and when you get out, we're going to start fresh and figure out how to stay connected to each other without jeopardizing our safety."

She nodded. "I would like that. I'm sorry about all the trouble I caused you."

I shrugged and smiled. "Trouble always seems to find me. I'm just glad that this time it brought me closer to you and Dante again."

We hugged and she was led off. I also stopped by to see Agnes soon after, asking her to look after Nat in whatever way possible. She promised she'd do what she could. Somehow, I suspected Agnes could make a lot happen around there if she put her mind to it.

I spoke with Dante next. "You gonna stick around or head off on a new adventure?"

"I can't leave Nat. We promised to stick together, through good and bad. I'll find some work and visit her as often as I can until she gets out. Then, we'll figure it out from there."

"You're a good friend. I don't suppose you can find some time to call me every once in a while?" I pulled him into a quick hug.

He tightened the embrace. "Call and maybe even watch a sunset or two with you. After all, I know where you live now."

I laughed. "Indeed, you do. And I plan to live there for a very long time."

"Maybe I'll even buy Nat some jewelry from your shop to celebrate when she gets out."

That reminded me I had selected a piece for her as well. I reached in my purse and handed it to him. "Will you give this to her for me when she gets out?"

He admired the piece for a moment, then handed it back to me. "Nah, you give it to her yourself. I think she would really like that."

"Deal. Stay safe, Dante, until we meet again."

He hugged me once more. "Until we meet again."

As I made my way to my truck, a free woman at last, my phone dinged. I opened the email from the Wilson CIA. The election results were in. My smile couldn't be subdued as I saw Tessa's name on those who had been elected. Alan Knightly had retained his spot, and much to my surprise, the third seat went to Jackie Price. This meant JB had not won his re-election bid, and Denise had also lost. My thought was that Denise would take it a whole lot better than JB. Only time would tell how this played out for the good citizens of Wilson, especially knowing Jackie might merely be a puppet for Karen.

I finished the day off at Pete and Kelsey's home. I'd brought tequila for Pete and jewelry for Kelsey, along with the check from the county clerk's office to return the bond money she'd fronted for me. Kelsey opened the door with my first knock and immediately pulled me into a hug. "I told you it would all work out."

She stepped back and let me in. "Well, you were right, as always."

"Don't go telling her that! She's already hard enough to live with," Pete teased from inside the house.

"Pete! Don't start." She laughed.

I walked into the living room and handed Pete another bottle of the good stuff. He admired it for a moment before asking, "You're not going to try to wheedle information out of me again, are you?"

I laughed. "No, not at all. This is a thank you gift for connecting me with JT."

"He's one of the best, for sure."

"You think James Cutter will try to hire him for his murder defense, along with any other number of charges being levied against him?"

Pete shook his head. "After being cut off from his family and their fortune, he's probably going to end up with a public defender."

"Guess he learned the hard way that crime doesn't pay."

"Well, it pays the attorneys." He laughed. "JT tells me you have him on retainer."

"I figure it's never a bad thing to have one of the good guys on your side, and since you wouldn't take the job..." I hedged, hoping he might share a bit more of his story.

The tequila bottle was stashed, and he pulled out the one that I'd given him last week. "We'll save that story for another time. For now, you're a free woman, my wife has her money back, and my firm is happy about the win and securing a new client."

"That certainly is something to celebrate. Are you suggesting a toast?" I noticed he was pouring the liquid into shot glasses.

"Sure am. Give me a minute to get the limes."

While he was in the kitchen, I handed a small gift bag to Kelsey. "What's this?"

"Just a little something to say thank you for always standing with me and calling me on my BS when necessary. That's what good friends do."

She blushed a shade of red brighter than her auburn hair. "That's what best friends do."

I nodded. "Best friends, for sure."

She opened the bag and pulled out the earrings. "Oh, Sadie. They're beautiful! Thank you."

"My pleasure." The joy on her face as she admired them was all the thanks I really needed. I secretly hoped Nat would love her gift as much when I gave it to her in six months.

Pete arrived and handed us each a glass. "Sadie, why don't you do the toast?"

I thought for a moment before raising my glass. "To friendship."

"To friendship," they both replied.

I enjoyed my good friends and the tequila, relishing the fact that, once again, I'd been able to defy the odds, survive the conspiracies, and most importantly, make sure that good triumphed over evil.

Acknowledgments

Special thanks to the wonderful citizens in my slice of heaven here in Texas who taught me how wonderful community can be and, through their sense of adventure and love of life, help provide inspiration for my stories.

Sending a shout out to the Windy City writing group that took an aspiring author and provided the necessary guidance, support, and care that other writers can uniquely give. I wouldn't have made it this far without you!

About the Author

USA Today Best-Selling author Nicole Leiren likes to have fun -- in life, with her characters and, of course, family and friends. A Midwesterner at heart, she now proudly calls South Texas her home and lives with her husband on a beautiful peninsula in Lake Conroe.

Nicole enjoys sharing the laughter, mystery, and occasionally a little mayhem she forces her characters to endure all for the reader's pleasure! Her stories allow you to take a break and immerse yourself in a page turning story until you reach the whodunit or happily ever after (usually both!)

facebook.com/NicoleLeirenAuthorPage

instagram.com/nicoleleiren

About the Publisher

Harbor Lane Books, LLC is a US-based independent digital publisher of commercial fiction, non-fiction, and poetry.

Connect with Harbor Lane Books on their website www.harborlanebooks.com and on social media @harborlanebooks.

facebook.com/harborlanebooks

x.com/harborlanebooks

instagram.com/harborlanebooks

tiktok.com/@harborlanebooks

threads.net/harborlanebooks

pinterest.com/harborlanebooks

bsky.app/profile/harborlanebooks.bsky.social

youtube.com/harborlanebooks

www.ingramcontent.com/pod-product-compliance
Lightning Source LLC
Chambersburg PA
CBHW061120310726
48974CB00002B/623